Abilene leaned close to him. "Don't you wish you'd done this sooner?" Her hair swung forward. He could smell her fresh, tart scent. He wanted to touch her hair. He wanted it bad.

And he had a thousand reasons why he shouldn't have what he wanted.

To hell with all those reasons.

He lifted his hand from the table and caught a thick lock between his fingers.

He wanted to kiss her, to feel the give, the texture, the heat of her mouth.

She said his name on a whisper of sound. And he thought that no one, ever, had said his name the way she did. With tenderness. And complete understanding.

With acceptance. And the sweet heat of honest desire.

There was nothing else, at that moment. Just Abilene.

So close to him, leaning closer…

Dear Reader,

Once, Donovan McRae was arguably the finest architect in America. He loved his work and he also enjoyed a reputation as a skilled and daring extreme sports enthusiast—a world-class ice climber. But in the past year, the formerly gregarious genius has completely shut himself off from the world. And no one knows why.

He hasn't been out of the gorgeous house, one he designed in the middle of the West Texas high desert a hundred miles from El Paso, in months. He's turned away friends and associates, refusing to see anyone—including Abilene Bravo, who had won the special fellowship he offered before he turned his back on his own life. She's been waiting a year for the important collaboration with him to begin.

No way can he put her off forever. Eventually, he has to let Abilene in.

And when he does, he's going to get more than he bargained for. The honest, forthright and optimistic Abilene is not about to let him hide from the world forever. Whether he likes it or not, she's determined to throw open some windows and doors and let the light in.

Sparks will fly. Guaranteed.

Happy reading everyone,

Christine Rimmer

DONOVAN'S CHILD

CHRISTINE RIMMER

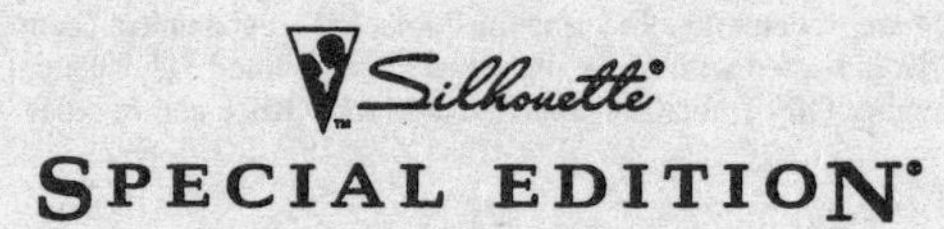

Published by Silhouette Books
America's Publisher of Contemporary Romance

ISBN-13: 978-0-373-65577-9

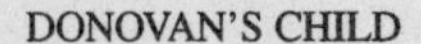

This edition published by arrangement with Harlequin Books S.A.

For questions and comments about the quality of this book please contact us at Customer_eCare@Harlequin.ca.

Visit Silhouette Books at www.eHarlequin.com

Printed in U.S.A.

Books by Christine Rimmer

Silhouette Special Edition

†*Married by Accident* #1250
Cinderella's Big Sky Groom #1280
A Doctor's Vow #1293
†*The Millionaire She Married* #1322
†*The M.D. She Had To Marry* #1345
The Tycoon's Instant Daughter #1369
†*The Marriage Agreement* #1412
†*The Marriage Conspiracy* #1423
*******His Executive Sweetheart* #1485
*******Mercury Rising* #1496
*******Scrooge and the Single Girl* #1509
††*The Reluctant Princess* #1537
††*Prince and Future...Dad?* #1556
††*The Marriage Medallion* #1567
§*Fifty Ways To Say...I'm Pregnant* #1615
§*Marrying Molly* #1639
§§*Stranded with the Groom* #1657
§*Lori's Little Secret* #1683
§*The Bravo Family Way* #1741
‡*The Reluctant Cinderella* #1765
§*Married in Haste* #1777
§*From Here to Paternity* #1825
‡‡*The Man Who Had Everything* #1838
§*A Bravo Christmas Reunion* #1868
§*Valentine's Secret Child* #1879
°*In Bed with the Boss* #1909
§*Having Tanner Bravo's Baby* #1927
§**The Stranger and Tessa Jones* #1945
§*The Bravo Bachelor* #1963
§*A Bravo's Honor* #1975
§*Christmas at Bravo Ridge* #2012
§*Valentine Bride* #2023
§*A Bride for Jericho Bravo* #2029
¶*McFarlane's Perfect Bride* #2053
§*Expecting the Boss's Baby* #2077
§*Donovan's Child* #2095

Silhouette Books

Fortune's Children
Wife Wanted
**The Taming of Billy Jones*
†*The Bravo Billionaire*
Montana Mavericks: Big Sky Brides
"Suzanna"
Lone Star Country Club
Stroke of Fortune
Lone Star Country Club: The Debutantes
"Reinventing Mary"

*The Jones Gang
†Conveniently Yours
**The Sons of Caitlin Bravo
††Viking Brides
§Bravo Family Ties
§§Montana Mavericks: Gold Rush Grooms
‡Talk of the Neighborhood
‡‡Montana Mavericks: Striking It Rich
°Back in Business
¶Montana Mavericks:
Thunder Canyon Cowboys

CHRISTINE RIMMER

came to her profession the long way around. Before settling down to write about the magic of romance, she'd been everything from an actress to a salesclerk to a waitress. Now that she's finally found work that suits her perfectly. Christine is grateful not only for the joy she finds in writing, but for what waits when the day's work is through: a man she loves, who loves her right back, and the privilege of watching their children grow and change day to day. She lives with her family in Oklahoma. Visit Christine at www.christinerimmer.com.

To all of you wonderful readers at eHarlequin
who encouraged me to write this book.
Thank you.

Chapter One

"Impress me," Donovan McRae commanded from behind a matched pair of enormous computer screens.

The screens sat on a desktop that consisted of a giant slab of ash-colored wood. The slab of wood was mounted on a base hewn from what appeared to be volcanic rock. The desk, the screens and the man were way down at the far end of a long, slant-roofed, skylit space, a space that served as Donovan's studio and drafting room in his sprawling, half-subterranean retreat in the West Texas high desert.

Impress me?

Abilene Bravo could not believe he'd just said that.

After all, she'd been imagining this moment for over a year now. At first with anticipation, then with apprehension and finally, as the months dragged by, with growing fury. She'd waited so long for this day—and the first words out of the "great man's" mouth were *Impress me?*

Hadn't she already done that? Wasn't that how she'd won this prize fellowship in the first place?

And would it have killed him to emerge from behind that fortress of screens, to rise from that volcano of a desk, to gesture her nearer, maybe even to go so far as to offer a handshake?

Or, hey. Just, you know, to say hello?

Abilene gritted her teeth and tamped her anger down. She reminded herself that she was not letting her big mouth—or her temper—get the better of her.

She did have something to show him, a preliminary design she'd been tinkering with, tweaking to perfection, for months as she waited for this all-important collaboration to begin. Donovan's assistant had led her to a workstation, complete with old-school drafting table and a desk, on which sat a computer loaded up with the necessary computer-assisted design software.

"Well?" Donovan barked at her, when she didn't respond fast enough. "Do you have something to show me or not?"

Abilene saw red, and again ordered her heart to stop racing, her blood not to boil. She said, in a voice that somehow stayed level, "I do, yes," as she shoved her memory stick into an empty port.

A few clicks of the mouse and her full-color introductory drawing materialized in front of her. On his two screens, Donovan would be seeing it, too.

"My rendering of the front elevation," she said.

"Self-evident," he grumbled.

By then, her hand was shaking as she operated the mouse. But beyond that slight tremor, she kept herself well under control as she began to show him the various views—the expanded renderings of classrooms, the central cluster of rooms for administration, the negative spaces that made up the hallways, the welcome area, the main entrance and vestibule.

She intended to cover it all, every square inch of the facility, which she had lovingly, painstakingly worked out—the playgrounds, the pool area, even the parking lot and some general landscaping suggestions. From there, she would go into her rough estimate on the cost of the project.

But she didn't get far. Ninety seconds into her presentation, he started in on her.

"Depressing," he declared darkly from behind his wall of monitors. "Institutional in the worst sense of the word. It's a center for underprivileged children, not a prison."

It was too much—all the months of waiting, the wondering and worrying if the fellowship was even going to happen. Then, out of nowhere, at last—the call.

That was yesterday, Sunday, the second of January. "This is Ben Yates, Donovan McCrae's personal assistant. Donovan asked me to tell you that he's ready to begin tomorrow. And to let you know that instructions will be sent via email...."

She'd had a thousand questions. Ben had answered none of them. He'd given her a choice. She could be flown to El Paso and he would pick her up there. Or she could drive her own vehicle.

She'd opted to drive, figuring it was better to have her own car in a situation like this. In order to arrive before dark, she'd been on the road before the sun came up that morning.

The drive was endless. An eight-hour trek across the wide-open, windblown desert to this godforsaken corner of Texas.

And now she was here, what? She'd met the great

man at last. And she found him flat-out rude. As well as dismissive of her work.

He demanded, "What were you thinking to bring me lackluster crap like this?"

Okay, worse than dismissive.

The man was nothing short of brutal. He'd seen a fraction of what she'd brought. And yet he had no compunction about cutting her ideas to shreds.

Abilene had had enough. And she said exactly that. "Enough." She closed her files and ejected her memory stick.

"Excuse me?" came the deep voice from behind the screens. He sounded vaguely amused.

She shot to her feet. Upright, at least she could see the top half of his head—the thick, dark gold hair, the unwavering gray-blue eyes. "I waited a very long time for this. But maybe you've forgotten that."

"I've forgotten nothing," was the low reply.

"We were to have started at the beginning of last year," she reminded him.

"I know when we were scheduled to start."

"Good. So have you maybe noticed that it's now January of the *next* year? Twelve months I've been waiting, my life put virtually on hold."

"There is no need to tell me what I already know. My memory is not the least impaired, nor is my awareness of the passage of time."

"Well, *something* is impaired. I do believe you are the rudest person I've ever met."

"You're angry." He made a low sound, a satisfied kind of sound.

"And that makes you *happy?*"

"Happy? No. But it does reassure me."

He found it *reassuring* that she was totally pissed off

at him? "I just don't get it. There's such a thing as common courtesy. You could at least have allowed me to finish my presentation before you started ripping my work apart."

"I saw enough."

"You saw hardly anything."

"Still. It was more than enough."

By then, she just didn't care what happened—whether she stayed, or whether she threw her suitcases back into her car and headed home to San Antonio. She spoke with measured calm. "I would really like to know what you were doing all year, that you couldn't even be bothered to follow through on the fellowship you set up yourself. There are kids out there who desperately need a center like this one is supposed to be."

"I know that." His voice was flat now. "You wouldn't be here now if I didn't."

"So then, what's up with you? I just don't get it."

Unspeaking, he held her gaze for a solid count of five. And then, bizarrely, without moving anything but his arms, he seemed to roll backward. His torso turned, his arms working.

He rolled out from behind the massive desk—in a wheelchair.

Chapter Two

A wheelchair.

Nobody had mentioned that he was using a wheelchair.

Yes, she'd heard that he'd had some kind of accident climbing some snow-covered mountain peak in some distant land. But that was nearly a year ago. She'd had no clue the accident was bad enough for him to still need a wheelchair now.

"Oh, God. I had no idea," she heard herself whisper.

He kept on rolling, approaching her down the endless length of the room. Beneath the long sleeves of the knit shirt he wore, she could see the powerful muscles of his arms bunching and releasing as he worked the wheels of the chair. He didn't stop until he was directly in front of her.

And then, for several excruciating seconds, he stared up at her as she stared right back at him.

Golden, she thought. He was as golden up close and personal as in the pictures she'd seen of him. As golden as from a distance, on a stage, when she'd been a starry-eyed undergraduate at Rice University and he'd come to Houston to deliver an absolutely brilliant lecture on form, style and function.

Golden hair, golden skin. He was a beautiful man, broad-shouldered and fit-looking. A lion of a man.

Too bad about the cold, dead gray-blue eyes.

He broke the uncomfortable silence with a shrug. "At least you're no doormat."

She thought of the apology she probably owed him. She really should have considered that there might be more going on with him than sheer egotism and contempt for others.

Then again, just because he now used a wheelchair didn't mean he had a right be a total ass. A lot of people faced difficult challenges in their lives and still managed to treat others with a minimum of courtesy and respect.

She returned his shrug. "I have a big mouth. It's true. And my temper rarely gets the better of me. But when it does, watch out."

"Good."

It wasn't exactly the response she'd expected. "It's good that I never learned when to shut up?"

"You've got guts. I like that. You can be pushed just so far and then you stand up and fight. You're going to need a little fighting spirit if you want to have a prayer of saving this project from disaster."

She didn't know whether to be flattered—or scared to death. "You make it sound as though I would be doing this all on my own."

"Because you *will* be doing this all on your own."

Surely she hadn't heard him right. Caught by surprise, she fell back a step, until she came up against the hard edge of the drafting table. "But..." Her sentence trailed off, hardly begun.

It was called a fellowship for a reason. Without his name and reputation, the project would never have gotten the go-ahead in the first place. The San Antonio Help the Children Foundation was all for giving a bright, young hometown architect a chance. But it was Donovan McCrae they were counting on to deliver. He knew that every bit as well as she did.

The ghost of a smile tugged at the corners of his perfectly symmetrical mouth. "Abilene. You're speechless. How refreshing."

She found her voice. "You're Donovan McCrae. I'm not. Without you, this won't fly and you know it."

"We need to carry through."

"You noticed. Finally."

A slow, regal dip of that leonine head. "I've put this off for way too long. And as you've already pointed out, there's a need for this center. An urgent need. So I'll...supervise. At least in the design phase. I'll put my stamp of approval on it when I'm satisfied with what you've done. But don't kid yourself. If it gets built, the design will be yours, not mine. And you will be following through in construction."

Abilene believed in herself—in her talent, her knowledge, and her work ethic. Yes, she'd hoped this fellowship would give her a leg up on snaring a great job with a good firm. That maybe she'd be one of the fortunate few who could skip the years of grunt work that went into becoming a top architect. But to be in charge of a project of this magnitude, at this point in her career?

It killed her to admit it, but she did anyway. "I don't know if I'm ready for that."

"You're going to have to be. Let me make this very clear. I haven't worked in a year. I doubt if I'll ever work again."

Never work again?

That would be a crime. She might not care much for his personality. But he was, hands down, the finest architect of his generation. They spoke of him in the same breath with Frank O. Gehry and Robert Venturi. Some even dared to compare him favorably to Frank Lloyd Wright. He blended the Modern with the Classical, Bauhaus with the Prairie style, all with seeming effortlessness.

And he was still young. Not yet forty. Many believed an architect couldn't possibly hit creative stride until at least the age of fifty. There was just too much to learn and master. Donovan McCrae's best work *should* be ahead of him.

"Never work again..." She repeated the impossible words that kept scrolling through her mind.

"That's right." He looked...satisfied. In a bleak and strangely determined sort of way.

"But why?" she asked, knowing she was pushing it, but wanting to understand what, exactly, had happened to him to make him turn his back on the kind of career that most would kill for. "I mean, there's nothing wrong with your *brain*, is there?"

An actual chuckle escaped him. "You *do* have a big mouth."

She refused to back off. "Seriously. Have you suffered some kind of brain damage?"

"No."

"Then why would you stop working? I just don't get it."

Something flashed in those steel-blue eyes of his. She sensed that he actually might give her an answer.

But then he only shook his head. "Enough. I'll take that memory stick." He held out his hand.

She kept her lips pressed together over a sarcastic remark and laid the stick in his open palm.

He closed his fingers around it. "Ben will show you to your rooms. Get comfortable—but not *too* comfortable." He backed and turned and wheeled away from her, disappearing through a door beyond the looming edifice that served as his desk.

"Abilene?" said a quiet voice behind her. She turned to face Ben Yates, who was slim and tall and self-contained, with black hair and eyes to match. "This way."

She grabbed her bag off the back of her chair and followed him.

The house was a marvel—like all of Donovan McCrae's designs. Built into the side of a rocky cliff, it had seemed to Abilene, as she approached it earlier, to materialize out of the desert: a cave, a fortress, a palace made of rock—and a house—all at the same time.

It was built around a central courtyard. The back half nestled into the cliff face. It had large glass doors and floor-to-ceiling windows all along the courtyard walls, giving access to the outside and great views of the pool and the harsh, beautiful landscaping. The facade side had windows and glass doors leading to the courtyard, as well. It also offered wide vistas of the wild, open desert.

Abilene's rooms were on the cliff side.

Ben ushered her in ahead of him. "Here we are."

The door was extra wide. The one to the bedroom was

wide, as well. She ran her hand down the rough-hewn doorframe.

Ben said, “Donovan had all the rooms made wheelchair-accessible, so it would be possible for him to get around anywhere in the house.”

She set her leather tote on a long table by the door and made a circuit. First of the sitting room, then of the bedroom. She looked into the walk-in closet where her own clothes were already hanging, and also the bathroom with its open shower and giant sunken tub.

The walls of the place seemed hewn of the rock face itself. And the furniture was rustic, made from twisted hunks of hardwood, starkly beautiful, like the desert landscape outside. French doors led out to the pool, and to the paths that wound through the courtyard.

Donovan’s assistant waited for her near the door. “The pool is yours to use as long as you’re here. There’s also a large gym downstairs. Check with me if you want to work out there and I’ll give you a schedule. Donovan uses the gym several hours a day and prefers to do so alone. The desk, computer and drafting table you used today in the studio are yours whenever you need them. Anytime you’re hungry, the kitchen is to your left as you exit your rooms. Just keep going until you reach it. Or you can ring. Press the red button on the phone. The housekeeper will answer and see that you get anything you need.”

“I know I’ll be very comfortable. Thank you.”

“I had your suitcases unpacked for you.”

She gave him a wry smile. “You assumed I would stay?”

“I did, yes.”

“I have to tell you, it was touch and go back there in the studio. Your boss can be rude.”

Apparently, Ben felt no obligation to leap to Donovan’s

defense. He spoke in his usual calm, unruffled tone. "Don't let him run you off."

"I won't. It's a promise."

"That's the spirit." Did he almost smile? She couldn't be sure. "Drinks at seven, just you and Donovan."

"That sounds really fun." She said it deadpan.

Ben took her meaning. "Only if you feel up to it. If you'd prefer, I can have something sent here, to your rooms."

"I definitely feel up to it."

"Excellent. If you follow either the courtyard breezeway or the interior hall in either direction, you'll eventually reach the front living room off the main entrance. Or you can simply cross the courtyard. It's chilly out, but not too bad."

"I'm sure I can find my way."

"Good, then. If you need anything—"

"I know. Press the red button on the house phone."

"I'll see you at dinner." He turned to go.

"Ben?"

He paused in the doorway, his back to her.

"I had no idea Donovan was in a wheelchair."

A silence. And then, reluctantly, he turned to her again. "Yes. Well, he's very protective of his privacy lately."

"A little communication goes a long way."

"You should be discussing this with him."

"Probably. What happened to him?"

Ben frowned. She was sure he would blow her off—or tell her again to ask Donovan. But then he surprised her and gave it up. "You may have heard about the ice-climbing accident."

"Just that there was one."

"He fell several hundred feet. Both legs sustained multiple fractures. His right tibia was driven up through the knee joint into the thigh."

She forced herself not to wince. "So…it's not his spine? I mean, he's not paralyzed?"

"No, he's not paralyzed."

"Will he walk again?"

"It's likely. But with…difficulty—and I've said more than enough. Seven. Drinks in the front living area."

And he was gone.

Abilene got out of her tired traveling clothes and jumped in the shower. In twenty minutes, she was freshened up and ready to go again. She considered exploring the house a little but decided to ask Donovan to show her around personally later. It might be a way to break the ice between them.

If such a thing was possible. The man was as guarded as they came. She had her work cut out for her, to try to get to know him a little.

Stretching out across the big bed, she stared up at the ceiling fixture, which consisted of tangled bits of petrified wood interwoven with golden globe-shaped lights that seemed strung on barbed wire. With a sigh, she let her eyes drift shut. Maybe what she really needed about now was a nice little nap….

The faint sound of her cell ringing snapped her awake. She went to the sitting room to get it. The display read Mom.

She answered. "I'm here. Safe. Don't worry."

"Just what I needed to know. Your father sends his love."

"Love to him, too. Did Zoe and Dax get away all right?" Saturday, which had been New Year's day, Abilene's baby sister had married her boss and the father of her coming baby. The newlyweds were to have left for their honeymoon on Maui that morning.

"They're on their way," her mother said. "Dax says to say hi to Donovan." Zoe's groom and Donovan were longtime acquaintances. "And your sister says to tell your new mentor that he'd better treat you right."

"I'll give him the message—both of them," Abilene promised.

"Have you...spoken with him yet?" Aleta Bravo asked the question carefully. She knew how upset Abilene had been with the whole situation.

"We spoke, yes. We...had words, I guess you could say. He was rude and dismissive. I was forced to tell him off."

"Should I be concerned?"

"Not as of now. I'll keep you posted."

"You can always simply come home, you know. It won't be that difficult to find a place for yourself. You're a Bravo. And you graduated at the top of your class."

"Mom. There are plenty of architects. But an architect who's worked closely with Donovan McRae, now that's something else altogether. A fellowship like this—one-on-one with the best there is—it just doesn't happen very often."

She considered adding that Donovan had been facing some serious challenges lately and possibly deserved a little slack for his thoughtless behavior. That he used a wheelchair now.

But no. Ben had made it painfully clear that McRae didn't want the world butting into his private business. She would respect his wishes. At least until she understood better what was going on with him.

Aleta said, "You're determined to stay, then?"

"Yes, I am."

"Well, then I suppose I won't be changing your mind…."

"No. You won't." And then, from her mother's end of the line, faintly, she heard the deep rumble of her father's voice.

Aleta laughed. "Your father says to give him hell."

"I will. Count on it."

After she said goodbye to her mom, she checked in with Javier Cabrera.

Javier was an experienced builder—and the first person she'd called when she got the summons yesterday from Ben. He owned his own company, Cabrera Construction, and had been kind enough to hire Abilene to work as a draftsperson on a few of his projects over the endless months she'd been waiting to get started on the fellowship. He'd even allowed her to consult with him at his building sites, giving her the chance to gain more hands-on experience in construction. He had become not only her friend, but something of a mentor as well.

His connections to her family were long-standing and complicated. Once the Bravos and the Cabreras had been mortal enemies. But now, in the past few years, the two families seemed to have more in common than points of conflict.

"Abby," Javier said warmly when he answered the phone. "I was wondering about you."

"I'll have you know I have made it safely to Donovan McRae's amazing rock house in the middle of nowhere."

"Did he tell you how sorry he was for all the time he made you wait and wait?"

"Not exactly."

"You get in your car and you come back to SA. I have work for you. Plenty of work."

She smiled at the driftwood and barbed-wire creation overhead. "You're good to me."

"I know talent. You will go far."

"You always make me feel better about everything."

"We all need encouragement." He sounded a little sad. But then, Javier *was* sad. He was still deeply in love with his estranged wife, Luz.

Abilene confided that Donovan had said her design was crap.

Javier jumped to her defense, as she had known that he would. "Don't listen to him. Your design is excellent."

"My design is…workmanlike. It needs to be better than that."

"You're too hard on yourself."

"I have to be hard on myself. I want to be the best someday."

"Stand tall," he said. "And call me any time you need to talk to someone who understands."

"You know I will."

They chatted for a bit longer. When she hung up, it was ten minutes of seven. She combed her hair and freshened her lip gloss and walked across the courtyard to the front of the house.

Donovan was waiting for her.

He sat by the burled wood bar, watching, as she approached the French doors from the courtyard.

She wore a slim black skirt, a button-down shirt with a few buttons left undone and a long strand of jade-colored beads around her neck. Round-toed high heels showed off her shapely legs, and her thick chestnut hair fell loose on her slim shoulders.

She pushed open one of the doors and stepped inside as if she owned the place. There was something about her that had him thinking of old movies, the ones made way back in the Great Depression. Movies in which the women were lean and tall and always ready with a snappy comeback.

From that first moment in the afternoon, when Ben ushered her into the studio, he had felt…annoyed. With her. With the project. With the world in general. He wasn't sure exactly why she annoyed him. Maybe it was all the energy that came off her, the sense of purpose and possibility that seemed to swirl around her like a sudden, bracing gust of winter wind.

Donovan didn't want bracing. What he wanted was silence. Peace. To be left alone.

But he had chosen her, sight unseen, by the promise in the work she'd submitted, before it all went to hell. And he would, finally, follow through on his obligation to the Foundation people. And to her.

They were doing this thing.

She spotted him across the room. Paused. But only for a fraction of a second. Then she kept coming, her stride long and confident.

He poured himself a drink and set down the decanter of scotch. "What can I get you?"

"Whatever you're having." She nodded at the decanter. "That's fine."

"Scotch? Don't women your age prefer sweet drinks?" Yeah. All right. It was a dig.

She refused to be goaded. "Seriously. Scotch is fine."

So he dropped ice cubes into a crystal glass, poured the drink and gave it to her, placing it in her long-fingered, slender hands. They were fine hands, the skin supple, the nails unpolished and clipped short. Useful hands.

She sipped. "It's good. Thanks."

He nodded, gestured in the direction of a couple of chairs and a sofa. "Have a seat." She turned and sauntered to the sofa, dropping to the cushions with artless ease.

He put his drink between his ruined legs and wheeled himself over there, rolling into the empty space between the chairs. "Your rooms?"

"They're perfect, thanks. Is it just you and Ben here?"

"I have a cook and a housekeeper—a married couple, Anton and Olga. And a part-time groundskeeper to look after the courtyard and the perimeter of the house." He watched her cross her pretty legs, admired the perfection of her knees. At least she was a pleasure to look at. "Did you rest?"

"I had a shower. Then my mother called. She told me to tell you that Dax sends his regards and my sister says you'd better be nice to me."

"Your sister and Dax…?"

"They were married on Saturday. And left on their honeymoon this morning."

"I hope they'll be very happy," he said without inflection. "And then what did you do?"

"Does that really matter to you?"

"It's called conversation, Abilene."

Her expression was mutinous, but she did answer his question. "After I talked to my mother, I called a… friend."

He took note of her hesitation before the word, friend. "A lover, you mean?"

She laughed, a low, husky sound that irked him to no end. A laugh that said he didn't intimidate her, not with his purposeful rudeness, nor with his too-personal questions. "No, not a lover. Javier is a builder. A really good one. I've been working for him over the past year, on and off. He also happens to be my half sister Elena's father. And the adoptive father of my sister-in-law, Mercedes."

He sipped his scotch. "All right. I'm thoroughly confused."

"I kind of guessed that by the way your eyes glazed over."

"Maybe just a few more details..."

She swirled her glass. Ice clinked on crystal. "My father and Javier's wife, Luz, had a secret affair years ago."

"An adulterous affair, that's what you're telling me."

"Yes. That's what I'm telling you. Luz was married to Javier. My dad to my mom. The affair didn't last long."

"Did your father love your mother?"

"He did—and he does. And I believe that Luz loved—and loves—Javier. But both of their marriages were troubled at the time."

"Troubled, how?"

She gave him a look. One that said he'd better back off. "I was a toddler when all this happened. I don't know all the details, all the deep inner motivations."

"Maybe you should ask your father."

"Maybe you should stop goading me."

"But I kind of like goading you."

"Clearly. Where was I? Wait. I remember. Javier—and everyone else except Luz—believed that Elena, my half sister, was his. But then, a few years back, the truth came out. It was...a difficult time."

"I would imagine."

"However, things are better now. Slowly, we've all picked up the pieces and moved on." She uncrossed her legs, put her elbows on her knees and leaned toward him. With the glass of scotch between her two fine hands, she studied him some more through those arresting golden-green eyes of hers. "So what did *you* do while I was busy talking on the phone?"

"Mostly, I was downstairs in the torture chamber with one of my physical therapists."

"You mean the gym? You were working out?"

"Torture really is a better word for it. Necessary torture, but torture nonetheless." And he had no desire to talk about himself. "What made you become an architect?"

She sank back against the sofa cushions. "Didn't I explain all that in my fellowship submission?"

As if he remembered some essay she had written to go with her original concept for the children's center. As if he'd even read her essay. Essays were of no interest to him. It was the work that mattered. "Explain it again. Briefly, if you don't mind."

She turned her head to the side, slid him a narrow look. He thought she would argue and he was ready for that—looking forward to it, really. But she didn't. "Four of my seven brothers work for the family company, BravoCorp. I wanted to be in the family business, too. BravoCorp used to be big into property development."

"And so you set out to become the family architect."

She gave him one slow, regal nod. "But since then, BravoCorp has moved more into renewable energy. And various other investments. There's not much of a need for an architect at the moment." She set her drink on the side table by the arm of the sofa. "What about your family?"

He put on a fake expression of shock. "Haven't you read my books?"

She *almost* rolled her eyes. "What? That was a requirement?"

"Absolutely."

"Well, then all right. I confess. I *have* read your

books. All four of them, as matter of fact. Will there be a quiz?"

"Don't tempt me. And if you've read my books, then you know more than anyone could ever want to know about my family."

"I'd like to hear it from you—briefly, if you don't mind." Those haunting eyes turned more gold than green as she gave his own words back to him.

He bent to the side and set his drink on the floor, then straightened in the chair and braced his elbows on the swing-away armrests. "I hate all this getting-to-know-you crap."

"Really? You seemed to be enjoying yourself a minute or two ago. But then, that was when you were asking the questions."

"You are an annoying woman." There. It was out.

She said nothing for several seconds. When she did speak, her voice was gentle. "You're not going to scare me off, Donovan. If you want me to go, you'll have to send me away—which means you'll also have to admit, once and for all, that you're backing out of the fellowship."

"But I'm not backing out of the fellowship."

"All right, then. Tell me about your family."

He was tempted to refuse. If she'd read his books as she claimed, she knew it all anyway. But he had the distinct impression that if he refused, she would only badger him until he gave it up.

So he told her. "My father was never in the picture."

From where he sat, without shifting his gaze from her face, he could see out the wide front windows. He spotted the headlights of a car approaching down the winding driveway. When the car pulled to a stop under the glow of the bright facade lights, he recognized the vehicle.

A red Cadillac.

He ignored the car and continued telling Abilene what she no doubt already knew. "My mother was a very determined woman. I was her only child and she set out to make me fearless. She was a force to be reckoned with. Adventurous. Always curious. And clever. It was her idea that I should write my autobiography when I wasn't even old enough to have one. She said I needed to cultivate myself as a legend and an authority. And the rest would follow. She died when I was in my early twenties. A freak skydiving accident."

Abilene had her elbow braced on the chair arm, her strong chin framed in the L of her thumb and forefinger. "A legend and an authority. I like that."

"It's a direct quote from my second book. If you really had read that book, you would remember it."

"This may come as a shock, but I don't remember everything I read."

"How limiting for you."

She gave him a slow smile, one that told him he was not going to break her. "Did you ever find your father?"

"To find him implies that I looked for him."

"So that would be a no?"

An atonal series of chimes sounded: the doorbell. Abilene sent a glance over her shoulder and shifted as if to rise.

"Don't get up," Donovan said.

"But—"

"Olga will take care of it."

Abilene sank back to the couch cushions as his housekeeper appeared in the wide-open arched doorway that led to the foyer. Olga cast him a questioning look. He gave a tight shake of his head.

Olga shut the thick archway doors before answering the bell. Seconds later, there were voices: Olga's and that of another woman. The heavy foyer doors blocked out the actual words.

He heard the front door shut.

And then Olga opened the doors to the living area again. "Dinner is ready," she announced, her square face, framed by wiry graying hair, serene and untroubled.

"Thanks, Olga. We'll be right in." Out in the driveway, the Cadillac started moving, backing and turning and then speeding off the way it had come. Abilene had turned to watch it go. He asked her, "Hungry?"

She faced him again. "Who was that?"

"Does it really matter? And more to the point, is it any of your business?"

Abilene stood and smoothed her skinny little skirt down over those shapely knees. "I can see this is going to be one long, dirty battle, every step of the way."

"Maybe you should give up, pack your bags, go back to San Antonio and your so-helpful builder friend, who also happens to be the father of your half sister, as well as of your sister-in-law. To the loving arms of your large, powerful, wealthy family. To your father, who loves your mother even though he betrayed her."

Her eyes went to jade, mysterious. Deep. "I'm going nowhere, Donovan."

"Wait. Learn. The evening is young yet. You can still change your mind."

"It's obvious that you don't know me very well."

Chapter Three

Dinner, Abilene found, was more of the same.

A verbal torture chamber. But at least it was brief. She saw to that.

Ben joined them in the dining room, which was the next room over from the enormous living area and had more large windows with beautifully framed views of the desert and distant, barren peaks.

There were several tables of varying sizes, as in a lodging house, or a bed-and-breakfast. They ate at one of the smaller ones, by the French doors to the courtyard, just the three of them. Olga brought the food and a bottle of very nice cabernet and left them alone.

Abilene asked, "Why all the tables? Are you thinking of renting out rooms?"

Donovan raised one glided eyebrow. "And this is of interest to you, why?"

Ben answered for him. "Once, Donovan thought he might offer a number of fellowships…."

Abilene smiled at Ben. At least he was civil. "Students, then?"

"Once, meaning long ago," Donovan offered distantly. "Never happened. Never going to happen. And I decided against changing the tables for one large one. Too depressing, just Ben and me, alone at a table made for twenty." He gave Ben a cool glance. "Ben is an engineer," he said. "A civil engineer."

Ben didn't sigh. But he looked as though he wanted to. "I had some idea I needed a change. I don't know what I was thinking. I was a very good engineer."

"I saved him from that," Donovan explained in a grating, self-congratulatory tone. "In the end, an architect knows something about everything. An engineer knows everything about one thing. It's not good for a man, to be too wrapped up the details."

Ben swallowed a bite of prime rib and turned to Abilene. "But then, my job here is to deal with the details. So I guess I'm still an engineer."

She sipped her wine. Slowly.

Donovan glared at her. "All right. What are you thinking?"

She set down her glass. "I'm thinking you need to get out more. How long have you been hiding out here in the desert?"

A low, derisive laugh escaped him. "Hiding out?"

She refused to let him off the hook. "Months, at least. Right? Out here a hundred miles from nowhere, with your cook and your housekeeper and your engineer."

"Are you going to lose your temper again?" he asked in that so-superior way that made her want to jump up and stab him with her fork.

"No. I'm not."

"Should I be relieved?"

She glanced to the side and saw that the corners of Ben's mouth were twitching. He was enjoying this.

Abilene wasn't. Not in the least. She was tired and she was starting to wonder if maybe she *should* do exactly what she'd told everyone she wouldn't: give up and head back to SA. "I'm just saying, maybe we could go out to dinner one of these nights."

"Go out where?" Donovan demanded.

"I don't know. El Paso?"

He dismissed her suggestion with a wave of his hand. "It's a long way to El Paso."

"It's a long way to anywhere from here."

"And that's just how I like it."

"I did go through a small town maybe twenty miles east of here today."

"Chula Mesa," said Donovan in a tone that said the little town didn't thrill him in the least.

Abilene kept trying. "That's it. Chula Mesa. And just outside of town, I saw a roadhouse, Luisa's Cantina? We could go there. Have a beer. Shoot some pool."

"I'm not going to Luisa's."

"You've been there before, then?"

"What does it matter? I'm not going there now. And as for Chula Mesa, there is nothing in that dusty little burg that interests me in the least."

"Maybe you could just pretend to be interested."

"Why would I do that?"

"Sometimes you have to pretend a little, Donovan. You might surprise yourself and find that you actually do enjoy what you're pretending to enjoy."

"When it comes to Chula Mesa, I'm not willing to

pretend. Wait. I'll go further. I'm not willing to pretend anywhere. About anything."

She really did want to do violence to him. To grab his big shoulders and shake him, at least. To tell him to grow up. Snap out of it. Stop acting like a very bright, very spoiled child. She took a bite of prime rib, one of potato. Dipped an artichoke leaf in buttery sauce and carefully bit off the tender end.

Donovan chuckled. "Fed up with me already, huh? I predict you're out of here by morning."

Ben surprised her by coming to her defense. "Leave her alone, Donovan. Let her eat her dinner in peace."

Donovan's manly jaw twitched. Twice. And then he grunted and picked up his fork.

They ate the rest of the meal in bleak silence.

When Abilene was finished, she dabbed at her lips with her snowy napkin, slid it in at the edge of her plate and stood. She spoke directly to Ben. "Would you tell the cook the food was excellent, please? I've had long day. Good night."

"I'll tell him," Ben replied pleasantly. "Sleep well."

"My studio," Donovan muttered. "Nine o'clock sharp. We have a lot of work to do."

She let a nod serve as her answer, and she left by the door to the interior hallway.

In her rooms, she changed into sweats and then sat on the bed and did email for a while. The house had wireless internet.

Really, it was kind of a miracle. Way out here, miles from nowhere, her cell worked fine and so did email and her web connection. She would have been impressed if she wasn't so tired and disheartened.

What she needed was sleep, but she felt restless, too.

Unhappy and unsatisfied. All these months of waiting. For this.

She knew if she got into bed, she would only lie there fuming, imagining any number of brutal ways to do physical harm to Donovan McRae.

Eventually, she turned on the bedroom TV and flipped through the channels, settling on The History Channel, where she watched a rerun of *Pawn Stars* and then an episode of *Life After People,* which succeeded in making her feel even more depressed.

Nothing like witnessing the great buildings of the world rot and fall into rubble after a so-enchanting evening with Donovan McRae. It could make a woman wonder if there was any point in going on.

At a few minutes after ten, there was a tap on her sitting room door.

It was Ben, holding two plates of something sinfully chocolate. "You left before dessert. No one makes flourless chocolate cake like Anton."

She took one of the plates and a fork and stepped aside. "Okay. Since there's chocolate involved, you can come in." She poked at the dollop of creamy white stuff beside the sinfully dark cake. "Crème fraîche?"

"Try it."

She did. "Wonderful. Your boss may deserve slow torture and an agonizing death, but I have no complaints about the food."

They sat on the couch and ate without speaking until both of their plates were clean.

"Feel better?" He set his plate on the coffee table.

She put hers beside it. "I do. Much. Thank you."

Ben stared off toward the doors to the darkened courtyard. "I started working for him two years ago, before the accident on the mountain. At the time, I really liked him. He used to be charming. He honestly did."

"I know," she answered gently. "I heard him speak once. He was so funny. Funny and inspiring. He made it all seem so simple. We were an auditorium full of students, raw beginners. Yet we came away feeling we were brilliant and accomplished, that we could do anything, that we understood what makes a building work, what makes it both fully functional and full of…meaning, too. Then, after he spoke, there was a party for the upperclassmen and professors, with Donovan the guest of honor. I was a freshman, not invited. But I heard how he amazed them all, how fascinating he was, how full of life, how…interested in everything and everyone. We all wanted to be just like him when we grew up."

"I keep waiting," Ben said, "for the day I wake up and he's changed back into the man he used to be. But it's been a while now. And the change is nowhere on the horizon."

She asked the central question. "So. What happened to him? Was it the accident on the mountain?"

Ben only smiled. "That, I really can't tell you. You'll have to find out from him."

She scoffed. "I don't think I'll hold my breath."

"He likes you."

That made her laugh. "Oh, come on."

"Seriously. He does. I know him well enough by now to read him a little, at least. He finds you fascinating. And attractive—both of which you are."

Was Ben flirting with her? She slid him a look. He was still staring off into the middle distance. So maybe not. "Well, if you're right, I would hate to see how he treats someone he *doesn't* like."

"He ignores them. He ignores almost everyone now.

Just pretends they aren't even there. Sends me or Olga to deal with them."

She gathered her knees up to the side. "This evening, before dinner, someone arrived and was sent away, someone in a red Cadillac. I didn't see who, but I heard a woman's voice talking to Olga at the door...."

Ben shrugged. "People come by, now and then. When they get fed up with him not returning their calls. When they can't take the waiting, the wondering if he's all right, the stewing over what could be going on with him."

"People like...?"

"Old friends. Mountain climbers he used to know, used to partner with. Beginning architects he once encouraged."

"Old girlfriends, too?"

"Yes." Ben sent her a patient glance. "Old girlfriends, too."

She predicted, "Eventually, they'll all give up on him. He'll get what he seems to be after. To be completely alone."

Ben's dark eyes gleamed. "With his cook and his housekeeper and his engineer."

She told him gently, "I didn't mean that as a criticism of you."

He smiled. A warm smile. "I know you didn't."

"I just don't get what's up with him."

"Well, don't worry. You're not the only one."

"How will he live, if he doesn't work? This house alone must cost a fortune to run."

"His books still make money."

"But an architect needs clients. We're not like painters or writers. We can't go into a room and lock the door and turn out a masterpiece and *then* try to sell it...."

"I know," Ben said softly. He admitted, "Eventually,

there could be a problem. But not for a few years yet, anyway…." There was a silence. Ben was gazing off toward the courtyard again.

Finally, she said, "You seemed pretty stuffy at first."

He chuckled. "Like the butler in one of those movies with Emma Thompson, right?"

"Pretty much. But now I realize you're not like someone's snobby butler, not in the least. You're okay, Ben."

He did look at her then. His dark eyes were so sad. "I was afraid, after the way he behaved at dinner, that he'd succeeded in chasing you off. I hope he hasn't. He needs a little interaction, with someone other than Anton, or Olga. Or me."

"A fresh victim, you mean."

"No. I mean someone smart and tough and aggressively optimistic."

"Aggressively optimistic? That's a little scary."

"I meant it in the best possible way."

"Oh, right."

"I meant someone able to keep up with him—I could use someone like that around here, too, when you come right down to it. Someone like you…"

"I wouldn't say I'm exactly keeping up with him."

"Well, I would."

She drooped back against the couch cushions. "Okay, I'm still here. But it's going to take a lot of chocolate, you know."

"I'll make sure that Anton keeps it coming." He got up. "And I'll let you get your rest."

She waited until he reached the door before she said, "Good night."

"'Night, Abilene." And he was gone.

* * *

"It's not a *horrible* arrangement of the space," Donovan announced when she entered the studio the next day. He was already at his desk, staring at his computer screens.

She saw that her design for the center was up on the computer at the desk she'd used the day before—which meant he was probably looking at the same thing on his two ginormous screens.

Just to be sure, she marched down the length of the room and sidled around to join him behind his desk.

Yep. It was her design. Up on display like a sacrificial offering at a summoning of demons. Ready to be ripped to shreds by the high priest of darkness.

He shot her an aggravated glance. "What? You do have a desk of your own, you know."

She sidled in closer, and then leaned in to whisper in his ear. "But yours is so much bigger, so much…more impressive."

He made a snarly sound. "Did I mention you annoy me?"

"Yes, you did. Don't repeat yourself. It makes you seem unimaginative." He smelled good. Clean. With a faint hint of some really nice aftershave. How could someone who smelled so good be such an ass?

It was a question for the ages.

"You're crowding me," he growled.

"Oh, I'm so sorry…." She straightened again, and stepped back from him, but only a fraction.

"No, you're not—and I don't like people lurking behind me, either."

"Fair enough." She slid around so she was beside him again, put her hand on his sacrificial slab of a desk and leaned in as close as before. "I slept well, surprisingly. And I'm feeling much better this morning, thank you."

He turned his head slowly. Reluctantly. And met her eyes. "I didn't ask how you slept."

"But you should have asked."

"Yeah. Well, don't expect a lot of polite noises from me."

She heaved a fake sigh. "I only wish."

"If you absolutely have to lurk at my elbow, pay attention." He turned back to the monitors, began clicking through the views. "Have you noticed?"

This close, she could see the hair follicles of his just-shaved beard. His skin was as golden and flawless from beside him as from several feet away. He must get outside now and then, to have such great color in his face. And his neck. And his strong, lean hands. "Noticed what?"

"It lacks a true *parti*." The *parti*, pronounced *par-TEE*, as in *We are going to par-tee*, was the central idea or concept for a building. In the process of creating a building design, the *parti* often changed many times.

She jumped to her own defense. "It does not lack a *parti*."

He sent her a look. "You never mentioned the *parti*."

"You didn't ask."

"Well, all right then. What *is* the *parti?*" He let out a dry chuckle. "Nestled rectangles?"

Okay, his guess was way too close. She'd actually been thinking of the *parti* as *learning rectangles*. Which somehow seemed ham-handed and far too elementary, now he'd taken his scalpel of a tongue to it.

"What's wrong with rectangles?" She sounded defensive and she knew it. "They're classrooms. Activity rooms. A rectangle is a perfectly acceptable shape for a classroom."

"Children deserve a learning space as open and receptive as their young minds."

"Oh, wait. The great man speaks. I should write that down."

"Yes, you should. You should carry a notebook around with you, and a pen, be ready to jot down every pearl of wisdom that drops from my lips." He spoke with more irony than egotism.

And she almost laughed. "You know, you are amusing now and then—in your own totally self-absorbed way."

"Thank you. I agree. And you need to start with some soft sketches. You need to get off the computer and go back to the beginning, start working with charcoal, pastels and crayons."

"Starting over. Wonderful."

"To truly gain control of a design," he intoned, "one must first accept—even embrace—the feeling that everything is out of control."

"I'm so looking forward to that."

"And we have to be quick about it. I told the Foundation we'd be ready to bring in the whole team in six weeks." He meant the builder, the other architects and the engineers.

"Did you just say that *we'd* be ready?"

"I decided it would be unwise to go into how I won't be involved past the planning stages."

"Good thinking. Since you know exactly how that would go over—it wouldn't. It won't. They're counting on *you*."

"And they will learn to count on you."

"So you totally misled them."

He looked down his manly blade of a nose at her. "Better that they see the design and the scale model and love it first, meet you at your most self-assured and persuasive.

You can give them a full-out oral presentation, really wow them. Make them see that you're not only confident, you're completely capable of handling the construction on your own."

"Confident, capable, self-assured and persuasive. Well. At least I like the sound of all that."

He granted her a wry glance. "You have a lot of work to do. Don't become *overly* confident."

"With you around? Never going to happen."

Loftily, he informed her, "March one is the target date for breaking ground."

She put up a hand, forefinger extended. "If I might just make one small point."

"As if I could stop you."

"I can't help but notice that suddenly, you're all about not wasting time. What's that old saying? *'Poor planning on your part does not constitute an emergency on mine.'*"

"The tight timeline has nothing to do with my planning, poor or otherwise."

"Planned or not, you're the one who kept us from going ahead months ago."

"Since you seem to be so fond of clichés, here's one for you. Can we stop beating the same dead horse? Yes, I put the project on hold. Now I'm ready to get down to work."

"And the timeline is impossibly tight."

"That may be so."

"How generous of you to admit it."

"But in the end, Abilene, there is only one question."

"Enlighten me."

"Do you want to make a success of this or not?"

Okay. He had it right for once. That *was* the question. "Yes, Donovan. I do."

"Then go back to your work area, get out your pastels, your charcoal, your fat markers. And stop fooling around."

Chapter Four

From that moment on, for Abilene, work trumped everything else. From nine—sometimes eight—in the morning, until after seven at night. Donovan supervised. He guided and challenged her. But he fully expected her to carry most of the load.

It would be her project in the truest sense. Which made it the chance of a lifetime for her, professionally. And also absolutely terrifying.

She drove herself tirelessly and mostly managed to keep her fear that she might fail at bay.

Donovan was not always there in the studio with her. He would set her a task or a problem to solve and then disappear, only to return hours later to check on her progress, to prod her onward.

Often during the day, when he wasn't with her, he took his personal elevator down to his underground gym to work with one of his physical therapists. Now and then, she would see them, Donovan's trainers. And the massage therapists, too. They were healthy, muscular types, both men and women. They came and went by the kitchen door. Anton, the cook, who was big and barrel-chested with a booming laugh and long gray hair clubbed back in a ponytail, would sometimes feed them after they finished putting Donovan through his paces.

Donovan seemed dedicated to that, at least, to taking care of his body, to making it stronger—though he continued to do nothing to heal his damaged spirit.

Or, apparently, his broken relationships. As had happened the first night, people Abilene never saw showed up at the front door to ask to speak with him. Olga or Ben always answered the doorbell when it rang. And they always sent whoever it was away.

More and more as the days went by, Abilene found herself wondering about that. About the people who cared for Donovan, the people he kept turning his back on. She would wonder—and then she would catch herself.

Really, it wasn't her concern if he refused to see former friends. She didn't even *like* him. Why should she keep wondering what had happened to him? Why couldn't she stop puzzling over what could have made him turn his back on other people, on a fabulous career?

There was the climbing accident, of course. That seemed the most likely answer to the question of what had killed his will to work, to fully engage in his own life. It seemed to her that *something* must have happened, something that had changed him so completely from the outgoing, inspiring man she'd admired from a distance back in college into someone entirely different.

She found she was constantly reminding herself that she was there to work, not to wonder what in the world had happened to Donovan McRae. She told herself to focus on the positive. If she could pull this off, create a design that would wow the Foundation people *and* hold her own overseeing construction, her career would be made.

And there were *some* benefits to being stuck in the desert with Donovan—Olga, for one.

The housekeeper was helpful and pleasant and ran the big house with seeming effortlessness. And beyond Olga, there was Anton's cooking; every meal was delicious and nourishing. And the conversation at dinner, while not always pleasant, did challenge her. Donovan might not be a very nice man, but he was certainly interesting. Ben provided a little balance, with his dry wit, his warm laughter.

Abilene really did like Ben. As the days passed, the two of them became friends. Every night, he came to her rooms for an hour or two before bedtime. Often, he brought dessert. They would eat the sweet treat, and he would commiserate with her over Donovan's most recent cruelties.

And beyond the great food, the comfortable house, the very efficient Olga and Abilene's friendship with Ben, there was music. Anton played the piano, and beautifully. Sometimes after dinner, in the music room at the east end of the house, he would play for them. Everything from Chopin to Gershwin, from Ray Charles to Norah Jones.

One night, about two weeks into her stay in Donovan's house, Anton played a long set of Elton John songs—songs that had been popular when Abilene's parents were young. Anton sang them, beautifully, in a smoky baritone, and Olga, who had a good contralto voice, sang harmony. Abilene felt the tears welling when they sang "Candle in the Wind."

She turned away, hoping Donovan wouldn't notice and torment her about it.

But it was never a good bet, to hope that Donovan wouldn't notice.

When the last notes died away, he went for the throat. "Abilene. Are you *crying?*"

She blinked the dampness away, drew her shoulders back and turned to him. "Of course not."

"Liar." He held her gaze. His was blue and cool and distant as the desert sky on a winter afternoon. "Your eyes are wet."

She sniffed. "Allergies."

He refused to look away. She felt herself held, pinned, beneath his uncompromising stare. She also found herself thinking how good-looking he was. How compelling. And how totally infuriating. "It's winter in the desert," he said. "Nobody has allergies now. You're crying. You protect yourself by pretending to be cool and sophisticated. But in your heart, you're a complete sentimentalist, a big bowl of emotional mush."

It occurred to her right then that he was right. And she wasn't the least ashamed of it. "Okay, Donovan. I plead guilty. I *am* sentimental. And really, what is so wrong with that?"

"Sentimentality is cheap."

Ben, sitting beside her, shifted tightly in his chair. "Cut it out, Donovan."

"Ben." She reached over and clasped his arm. "It's okay."

He searched her face. "You're sure?"

"I am positive." She turned her gaze on Donovan. "A lot of things are cheap. Laughter. Honest tears. Good times with good friends. A mother's love. A baby can have that love by the mere fact of its existence. Of its very vulnerability, its need for affection and care. Cheap is not always a bad thing—and I'll bet that when you were a child, you used to pull the wings off of butterflies." She regretted the dig as soon as it was out. It wasn't true and she knew it. Whatever had shriveled his spirit had happened much more recently than his childhood.

He totally surprised her by responding mildly. "I was a very nice little boy, actually. Sweet-natured. Gentle. Curious."

The question was there, the one that kept eating at her. She framed it in words. "So then, what is it, exactly, that's turned you into such a bitter, angry man?"

He didn't answer. But he did look away, at last.

And for the rest of the evening, he was quiet. The few times he did speak, he was surprisingly subdued about it, almost benign.

Ben brought her red velvet cake that night. "I figured you deserved it, after that dustup in the music room."

"It wasn't so bad, really. I shouldn't have said that about him torturing butterflies."

"It got him to back off, didn't it?"

"Yeah. But..."

"What?"

"I don't know. Sometimes, in the past few days especially, I don't feel angry with him at all. I only feel sorry for him."

Ben put on a frown. "So then you don't want this cake...."

She grabbed for it, laughing. "Don't you dare take that away."

He handed over one of the plates and she gestured him inside. They sat on the couch as they always did when he brought dessert.

She took a couple of slow, savoring bites. "I don't know how Anton does it. Red velvet cake always looks so good, you know? But as a rule, it's a disappointment."

He nodded. "I know. It's usually dry. And too sweet."

"But not Anton's red velvet cake." She treated her mouth to another slow bite. "Umm. Perfect. Moist. And the cream cheese frosting is to die for. So good..."

Ben laughed. "You should see your face."

"Can you tell I'm in heaven? Good company *and* a really well-made red velvet cake. What more is there to life?"

"You're happy. I like that."

She gave him a bright smile, ate yet another dreamy bite of the wonderful cake. "You know, we really should go into that little town, Chula Mesa, one of these nights."

He swallowed, lowered his fork. His dark eyes shone. "We?"

"Yeah. You. Me. Donovan."

"Donovan." Ben spoke flatly now. "Of course, Donovan."

"No, really. I think it would be good for him, for all three of us, to get out of this house for a while. We could invite Anton and Olga, too. Make it a group outing."

Ben wasn't exactly jumping up and down with excitement at the prospect of a night out with his boss. "Have you brought this up to him?"

"Just that first night." She made a show of rolling her eyes. "You remember how well that went."

"What can I say? You can't make him do what he doesn't want to do."

"Ben, he needs to get out. He's...hiding here. He's made this house into his fortress—you know that he has. It's not good for him."

Ben lowered his half-finished plate to his lap. "Listen to you. You're getting way too invested in him."

"What's wrong with that? You said it yourself, that first night. You said he needed someone like me around."

"I didn't mean that you should make him into a... project."

"But I'm not."

"Abilene. You're his protégé. Not his therapist."

"Which is a very good question. Does he *have* a therapist—a counselor I mean, someone to talk to? If he spent half as much time trying to figure out what's going on inside him as he does in the gym downstairs, he'd be a much happier person. Not to mention, more fun to be around."

"No. He doesn't have a counselor."

"Well, he should. And he should get out. We should work together on this, you and me, make it a point to get him to—"

"Abilene. Stop." Ben set his plate down, hard.

She blinked. "What?"

"*I'll* go with you, okay?" He spoke with intensity. With passion, almost. "Into Chula Mesa, to Luisa's. We can have a few drinks. A few laughs, just the two of us."

Just the two of us.

Suddenly, the rich cake was too much. She set it down, half-finished, next to Ben's. "Ben, I..."

He sat very still. And then he smiled. It was not a particularly pleasant smile. "Not interested, huh?"

"Ben..."

His lip still curled. But now, not in any way resembling a smile. "Just answer the question."

There was no good way to say it. "No. I'm not. Not in *that* way."

He let out a slow breath, and then smoothed his hair

back with both hands. "Well, at least you didn't say how much you *like* me. How much you want to be *friends.*"

"But, I do. On both counts. You know I do." She wanted to touch him. To soothe him. But that would be beyond inappropriate, given the circumstances. "But my liking you and wanting to be your friend…neither of those is the issue right now, is it?"

"No, they're not. The issue is that I want more. And you don't." Now he looked openly angry. "It's Donovan, right?"

She gaped. "Donovan? Not on your life."

He grunted, nodded his head. "Yeah. It's Donovan."

"Ben. Come on. I don't even *like* him."

"Yeah. You do. You like him a lot." He stood. "I think that you and I need to redefine the boundaries."

She hated that. But he was right. "Yes. I agree. I think we do."

"If you want to know about Donovan, you should ask him yourself. If you want to go to Chula Mesa with him, tell him so. If you think he needs a shrink, say so. Say it to him. Leave me out of it. Please."

He left her, shutting the door a little too loudly behind him.

"What did you do to Ben?" Donovan demanded when she walked into the studio the next morning bright and early.

As if she was answering that one. "Why do you ask?"

"Oh, come on. I know he's got a thing for you."

She took a careful breath. Let it out slowly. "If you knew that, you might have mentioned it to me before now."

"I thought it was none of my business."

"Oh, right. Because you're so considerate of other people and all." She was standing in front of her drafting table.

He rolled out from behind his twin computer screens and came at her, fast, stopping cleanly a foot from her shoes. "He left a half hour ago."

Her throat clutched. She gulped. "What do you mean, left?"

"He packed his suitcases and he left. He said he needed to get out of this house, away from here. Far away."

"For...how long?"

Donovan blew out a breath. "Abilene. He quit."

She felt awful. Yes, Ben had been upset last night. But she'd never imagined he would just pack up and move out, just walk away from a job he'd had for two years now. "But where will he go?"

Donovan stared up at her. His sky-colored eyes, as always, saw far too clearly. "If you cared that much, you wouldn't have turned him down when he made his play, now would you?"

She eased backward, around the drafting table, and sank into the swivel chair behind it, not even caring that Donovan would see the move for what it was: a retreat. "How would you know if he made a play for me?"

He let out a low sound—dismissive? Disbelieving? She couldn't tell which. "I guessed. And since you're not denying it, I'm thinking I guessed right."

She threw up both hands. "What do you want me to say?"

"How about the truth?"

"Fine. All right. He did ask me out. I said no." She glared at him, daring him to say one more word about it.

He said nothing. He only sat there, his strong hands gripping the wheels of his chair, watching her face.

She dropped her hands, flat, to the drafting table, making a hard slapping sound. "Where will he *go,* Donovan?" Tears of frustration—and yes, guilt, too—tried to rise. She gulped them down, hard.

He rolled a fraction closer and spoke with surprising gentleness. "Stop worrying. He owns a house in Fort Worth, near his family. And he's an excellent engineer. I gave him a glowing letter of recommendation. He'll easily find another job. Plus, it wasn't just you. I think he was getting a little tired of things around here. A little tired of the isolation, of dealing with me. He was ready to move on. And he definitely has options as to what to do next. So please, take my word on it, Ben is going to be fine."

She stared at him, vaguely stunned. He had just been *kind* to her, hadn't he? He'd made a real effort to soothe her worries about Ben.

Had he ever once been kind to her before?

Not that she recalled. And Donovan McRae being kind...that was something she would definitely have remembered.

She pressed her hands to her flushed cheeks, murmured softly, "It's...kind of you, to say that."

"Not kind," he answered gruffly. "It's only the simple truth."

A weak laugh escaped her. "You just can't stand it, can you? To have someone call you kind?"

"Because I'm not kind. I'm a hardheaded SOB with absolutely no consideration for anyone but myself. We both know that."

She closed her eyes, pressed her fingertips against her shut eyelids and wished she could quit thinking about the things Ben had said last night—about how she had a thing for Donovan. About how, if she had questions for

Donovan, she should gut up and ask them of the man himself.

Well, she absolutely did *not* have a thing for Donovan. Not in the way Ben had meant. She was only…intrigued by him. She was curious about him.

And yes, she wanted to help him get past whatever was eating at him, whatever had made him turn his back on his own life.

Was that so wrong?

He was watching her. Way too closely. "All right." He pulled a very clever sort of wheelie maneuver, leaning back in the chair, so the wheels lifted a fraction, turning while the wheels were lifted, and then rolling the chair backward until he was sitting beside her at the drafting table. "What terrifying thoughts are racing through that mind of yours?" He almost sounded…friendly.

So she told him. "I think you need someone to talk to."

"About what?"

"About…all the stuff that's bothering you. I think you need to see a trained professional."

He craned away from her in the chair. "A psychiatrist. You think I need a shrink."

"I do. Yes."

"No."

"Just like that?" She raised a hand and snapped her fingers. "No?"

"That's right. Just like that."

"Donovan, you're a very intelligent man. You have to know that there's no shame in seeking help."

"I didn't say there was shame in it. I only said no. And since I am perfectly sane and a danger to no one, I have that right. I'm allowed to say no."

"It's not about being sane. I know you're sane."

"That's a relief." He pretended to wipe sweat off his brow.

"I just thought that if you could talk it out with a professional, if you could—"

"I'll say it once more, since you have a bad habit of not listening when I say things the first time. No."

She could see she was getting nowhere on the shrink front. So she moved on to the next issue. "Then how about this? Will you go into Chula Mesa with me some evening?"

He actually groaned. "Didn't I make it clear two weeks ago that I was not going to Chula Mesa—with you, or otherwise?"

"You could rethink that. You could change your mind. People do that, you know, change their minds?"

"Abilene. Have you ever been in Chula Mesa?"

"Well, besides driving through it, no, I haven't."

"I've been in Chula Mesa. I've seen it all, been there. Done that. I don't need to go there again."

"Just…think about it. Please."

"I fail to understand what a visit to Chula Mesa could possibly accomplish."

"We'll get out of the house, see other people, broaden our horizons a little."

"If I wanted a broader horizon, I wouldn't look for it in Chula Mesa."

She was becoming irritated with him again. "You really should stop saying mean things about Chula Mesa."

"I will be only too happy to. As soon as you stop trying to drag me there."

"I'll leave it alone for now, okay? I'll bring it up again later."

"Why is it I don't find that comforting in the least?"

She still had a thousand unanswered questions for him. "One more thing..."

"With you, it's never just one more thing."

"Tell me about what happened, on that mountain, when you broke both your legs."

He slumped back in the wheelchair. "It's barely nine in the morning and already, you've exhausted me."

"Please. Tell me. I do want to know."

"You should have asked Ben, before you broke his heart."

She wanted to slap him. But then, that was nothing new. She schooled her voice to an even tone and reminded him, "A moment ago, you said he left more because of you than of me. Now you say I broke his heart."

"Figure of speech."

"Hah. Right—and since you brought it up, I'll have you know that I *did* ask Ben, that very first day. He told me that you fell several hundred feet down the side of a mountain, that both of your legs were badly damaged in the fall, each sustaining multiple fractures. He also said there *was* a possibility you might someday walk again."

"I can already walk." He smiled in a very self-satisfied way. "Your mouth is hanging open."

She snapped it shut. "But if you can walk...?"

"The chair is much more efficient," he explained. "And you have to understand that when I say I can walk, I mean with crutches. And also with considerable pain. Slowly, I'm improving. Very slowly."

"Well. That's good, right? That's excellent. What mountain was it, where?"

"What difference does the mountain itself make?"

"I would just like to know."

"We do eventually need to work today." He spoke in an infinitely weary tone.

"What do you mean, 'we'? Last I checked, all the work was on me. What mountain?"

He shook his golden head. "I can see it will take more energy to keep backing you off than to simply answer your unnecessary question."

"What mountain?"

"It's called Dhaulagiri." He pronounced it *doll-a-gear-ee.* "Dhaulagiri One. It's in Nepal, in the Himalayas. The seventh highest peak in the world. It's known as one of the world's deadliest mountains. Of all who try to reach the summit, forty percent don't come back. At least, not alive."

"So of course, you had to try and climb it."

"Is that a criticism?"

"No. Just an observation. So what happened—I mean, after you fell?"

"My climbing partner managed to lower himself down to me. And then, with him dragging me and me hauling myself along with my hands as best I could, we ascended again, to a more stable spot. He dug the ice cave. I wasn't much help with that. He dragged me in there. After that, he had to leave me to get help. That's a big no-no, in the climbing community. You never leave your partner. But we both agreed it was the only way, that since both of my legs were out of commission, there was no possibility I could make it down with only him to help me. So he made the descent without me. I was fortunate in that the weather held and a successful helicopter rescue was accomplished—but only after I spent three days alone on the mountain."

"In terrible pain," she added, because he didn't. "And is that it, then, those three horrific days? Are they why you say you won't work again, why you've retreated from the world?"

He studied her face for several very uncomfortable seconds, before he demanded, "What does it matter to you? What difference can it possibly make in your life, in the work that I'm perfectly willing to help you with, in the things I'm willing to teach you about the job I know you love?"

"Donovan, I want to understand."

He watched her some more. A searching kind of look. And then he said, "No."

She didn't get it. "No, you won't tell me?"

"No, it wasn't the three days in the ice cave—not essentially."

"So you're saying that *was* part of it, right?"

"No, that's not what I said."

"But if you—"

He put up a hand. "Listen. Are you listening?"

She pressed her lips together, nodded.

"If I'm a different man than I was a year ago…" He spoke slowly, as if to a not-very-bright child. "…it's not about my injuries. It's not about how I got them or how much they hurt. And it's not about the endless series of surgeries that came after my rescue, not about adapting to life on wheels. Society may ascribe all kinds of negative values to my situation, may view what happened to me when I fell down the mountain as a tragedy, blow it up all out of proportion to the reality, which is that I survived and I'm learning to live in my body as it is now."

She couldn't let that stand. "But Donovan, you're not learning to live, not in the truest sense. You're still… angry and isolated. You have Olga turn people away at the front door, people who care about you, people who have to be suffering, wondering what's going on with you."

He grunted. "Since you don't even know who those people are, how would you know that they're suffering?"

"You turn them away without even seeing them. That's just plain cruel. And on top of all the rest, you never intend to work again. *That* is a crime."

"Don't exaggerate."

"I'm not exaggerating. It *is* a crime, as far as I'm concerned. It's not right. Work is important. Work is...what we do."

"We?" He tried really hard to put on an air of superiority.

She wasn't letting him get away with that. "Yes, we. People. All people. We work. We all need that. Purposeful activity. Especially someone like you, who is the absolute best at what he does."

"You're going too far." His voice was low, a rumble of warning. "Way too far. You have no idea what I need. What I *have* to do."

"Well, all right. Then tell me. Explain it to me."

"Let it go, Abilene."

"But I want—"

He cut her off. "What *you* want. Yes. All, right. Let me hear it. You tell me what you want."

"I want to understand."

He leaned in closer to her. His eyes were the dark gray of thunderheads. "Why?"

"Well, I..." She was just too...aware of him. Of the scent of him that was turbulent, somehow. Fresh and dangerous, like the air before a big storm.

He prodded her. "Answer me."

"Because I..." She couldn't go on. All at once, she

realized she wasn't sure. Not of what she really wanted. And certainly not of what was actually going on here.

"Leave it alone," he said low. And then he wheeled away from her, swinging the chair effortlessly around the jut of her drafting table and out into the room. Halfway to his own desk, he spun on her again. "Will you just leave it now?"

She stared across the distance between them. And for no reason she could fathom, she felt her face flood with heat. And she felt guilty, suddenly. Guiltier even than when he told her that Ben had gone. She felt thoroughly reprehensible now, as if she'd been sneaking around somewhere she had no right go to, peering into private places, touching secret things.

"All right," she said, the words ragged-sounding, barely a whisper. "I'll leave it alone. For now."

"Leave it alone once and for all. Please." He waited for her to say that she would.

But she didn't answer him. She gave him no agreement, no promise that she would cease trying to learn about him, to understand him.

She couldn't make that kind of promise.

She couldn't tell that kind of lie.

Chapter Five

Donovan needed distance.

The painful conversation in the studio the morning that Ben quit was too much. He never should have let that happen between him and Abilene, and he set about making sure that nothing like it would happen again.

During work hours, he took care to set himself apart from her, to be only what he actually was to her: a teacher, the one who had set himself the task of helping her accomplish her goal. She was in his house for one reason—to get the design for the children's center ready to be presented to the Help the Children Foundation.

He was not her friend, he reminded himself repeatedly. They were not equals. She had a task to accomplish with his guidance. And that was all.

She did him the courtesy of letting him claim the distance he needed. He was on guard constantly, waiting for her to step over the line again, to badger him under the guise of trying to "understand" him.

But she didn't. She worked and she worked hard.

In the evening, all that week, by tacit agreement, they skipped the usual cocktails in the sitting area. They saw each other in the dining room, for dinner. They spoke of the progress that had been made on the design.

After they'd eaten, they said good-night.

He placed an ad in the local weekly paper, the *Chula Mesa Messenger,* for a new assistant. No, he didn't hold out much hope that he'd get an acceptable applicant that way. But he gave it a try.

The ad appeared when the paper came out on Thursday. Friday morning, four days after Ben's departure, he had three replies. He held the interviews that day.

One of the applicants seemed worth giving a trial. Her name was Helen Abernathy, and she was a retired secretary from Austin. Helen agreed to start that following Monday. She preferred not to live in, to return nightly to her own house and her retired husband, Virgil.

Helen's living at home was no problem for Donovan. He didn't really need a live-in assistant anymore, anyway. He'd become reasonably adept at taking care of himself by then. He could get into the shower by himself, dress himself, even drive himself in the specially modified van he'd bought, should he ever want to go anywhere. He only needed someone to handle correspondence, to pay the bills and field phone calls.

Since Helen would be going home at six, that would leave only him and Abilene at dinner. And when she returned to San Antonio, which would be in three weeks now, if all went as planned, he would eat alone.

That was fine with him. Perfect. It was the choice he had made.

* * *

Saturday, Abilene knocked off work at about four.

Donovan knew she would use the pool, which he kept heated in the winter. Lately, she'd been swimming every day after she finished working.

Donovan knew this because he'd happened to be in his rooms around five on the afternoon of the day Ben quit. He glanced out the French doors of his sitting room—and saw her by the pool.

He watched her swim that day.

And each day since.

She wore a plain blue tank suit, a suit that showed off the clean, sleek lines of her body. She had slim hips and nice breasts, breasts that were beautifully rounded, high and full—but not too full. The breasts of a woman who had yet to bear a child.

He admired her pretty body in the same way that he admired her spirit and her quick mind. Objectively. From the safe cocoon of his own isolation. He felt no desire when he watched her. It wasn't sexual. It was simple appreciation of the beauty of her healthy, young female form.

When she emerged from her rooms, she would toss her towel on a bench and dive right in. She would swim the length of the pool, turn underwater, and swim back to where she had started, turn again, and head back the other way.

Back and forth, over and over. She swam tirelessly.

After twenty minutes or so, she would emerge, breathing hard. She would towel off quickly, and disappear into her rooms again.

That Saturday afternoon, when she climbed from the pool, as she was reaching for the towel she'd left thrown across a stone bench, she paused. She turned her head until it seemed to him she was looking directly at him, where he sat in his chair just inside the French doors.

She simply stood there, water sliding off her slim flanks, her hair slicked close to her head. She stood there and she stared right at him through those eyes that seemed fully golden right then, not so much as tinged with the faintest hint of green.

He knew she couldn't see him, that the light was wrong—and so what if she did see him? It wasn't any big deal, that he had seen her swimming.

Still, he rolled his chair backward until he was out of her line of sight.

Dinner was at seven-thirty, as usual. He went to the dining room with apprehension tightening his chest, sure she was going to give him a hard time about spying on her while she swam.

But when she joined him, she seemed the same as always—or at least, the same as she had been since they'd both said too much on the morning Ben left. She was quiet. Polite. Professional. They spoke of the project. They agreed that it was going well.

Olga was just clearing off to bring the dessert when the doorbell rang. The housekeeper straightened from gathering up the dirty dishes.

Abilene leaped to her feet. "It's okay, Olga. I'll get the door." She spoke to the housekeeper—but she was looking straight at him. Daring him. Challenging him.

Olga hovered in place at the edge of the table, not sure what to do next.

So be it, he thought. "All right, Abilene. Go ahead. Get the door."

It was almost worth having to deal with whoever waited outside, to see the look of surprise on her face, the frank disbelief that he was finally going to let someone else in the house.

Olga calmly went back to clearing off.

And Abilene disappeared through the archway into the living area and the front hall beyond.

Abilene opened the door.

On the other side stood a pretty woman with thick black hair that fell in shining curls to below her shoulders. Small and shapely, the woman wore snug skinny jeans, a tight sweater and very high heels. She might have been thirty, or forty. Hard to tell. Behind her, in the dusty turnaround in front of the house, a red Cadillac waited—no doubt the same Cadillac Abilene had seen the night she first came to Donovan's house.

"Hello. I'm Luisa. Luisa Trias."

"Abilene Bravo." She shook the woman's offered hand. "I'm working with Donovan for a few weeks. Come on in…"

Luisa eased her fingers free of Abilene's hold and moved back a step. "Is Donovan here?"

"He is, yes. In the dining room. We're about to have dessert. Join us, why don't you?"

"Oh, I don't want to butt in. I only want to know that he's all right. I've driven out here twice before. Both times, I was told that he wasn't at home…."

Abilene hesitated. Really, how much did she have a right to say? Maybe jumping up and insisting that she would answer the doorbell hadn't been such a brilliant move, after all.

But then Donovan spoke from behind her. "Luisa. How are you?" Abilene glanced over to see him sitting in the archway to the living area.

The pretty black-haired woman gasped. Clearly, she'd

had no idea that he was using a wheelchair now. But Abilene had to hand it to her. She recovered quickly.

The woman scowled at him. "I've been calling. You never call back. And I've been out here, to try to see you. Your housekeeper keeps sending me away."

"I'm sorry, Luisa. Truly." He actually sounded remorseful. "I haven't been feeling like seeing anyone lately."

"Lately? It's been months since you came back." The huge dark eyes grew just a little misty. "A friend is a friend. You should know that. How is it that you've become such a bastard, Donovan? A big, selfish bastard, who cares so little for those who care for him?"

He had the grace to look ashamed. "It's a long story. Too long."

She touched the gold crucifix at her throat. "Are you all right?"

"I am. I'm fine. I promise you." He spoke gently, with what sounded to Abilene like real concern for Luisa's feelings. "Come in. Have some crème brûlée with us."

Luisa looked at him sideways. "I shouldn't forgive you…."

His smile was rueful. "Please. Come in."

"Are you sure? I needed to know that you're all right, but we can speak later if you—"

He put up a hand. "I repeat, crème brûlée. *Anton's* crème brûlée."

Finally, Luisa allowed herself to be convinced. She joined them in the dining room, where Olga served the dessert and coffee.

Luisa ate with relish. "Ah. Anton. That man can cook. Someday, when I open a real restaurant, I might have to steal him away from you."

"Luisa owns the local roadhouse, Luisa's Cantina,"

Donovan explained. He glanced fondly at the dark-haired woman. "It's a couple of miles outside of Chula Mesa."

Abilene sipped her coffee. "You mean the roadhouse I keep trying to get you to go to?"

He turned his gaze to her, his expression cool now. "That would be the one."

Luisa laughed, a husky, sexy sound. "Yes. It's a good idea, Abilene. Why don't you both come? And soon."

"We'll see," said Donovan. "One of these days…"

Abilene set down her coffee cup. It clinked against the saucer. "*I'll* be there next Friday night. Count on it—whether I can talk Donovan into coming with me, or not."

Luisa grinned. "Good. I'll look forward to seeing you." She sent Donovan a look from under her thick, black lashes. "You, too. I mean it. You've been acting like a stranger for so long now. It's time you stopped that."

"Luisa. I get the message. You can quit lecturing me."

"Come with Abilene, Friday night."

He looked away. "I'll think about it."

Luisa clucked her tongue. "I've been tending bar for almost two decades. I know what it means when a man says he'll think about something. It means that he's already done whatever thinking he is willing to do—and the answer is no."

He set down his spoon. "Enough about Friday night."

Even as he gruffly ordered Luisa to back off, there was real affection in his tone, in his expression. And Luisa seemed so fond of him, too.

Abilene knew she ought to make her excuses and go, give them a little privacy. No doubt the two of them wanted some time together, had things to say to each other that they wouldn't feel comfortable saying with someone else in the room.

Yet for reasons she refused to examine, she felt a certain reluctance to go, to leave him alone with a good-looking woman, a woman who'd most likely once been his lover.

Who might still be. Or plan to be.

Or...

Well, whatever the situation between the two of them was, exactly, Luisa and Donovan probably wanted some time to themselves.

She made herself rise. "I'm sure you two have a lot to catch up on, and I'll just—"

Luisa cut her off with another husky laugh. "Sit down, chica. It's not that way." She sent Donovan a teasing look. "Tell her. Make her see."

He made a gruff sound, something midway between a grunt and a chuckle. "Luisa's right. It's not that way. Though I did give it my best shot, back in the day."

Luisa made a face at him. "We met nine years ago, when he came out here to build this house. He came in my bar often then. And he was a big flirt. But I explained to him that I'm no longer a wild, foolish girl. I don't need a man to sweep me off my feet and then break my heart. But I can always use a true friend. And so we became friends—or so I thought." The corners of Luisa's full mouth drew down. "Until you stopped taking my phone calls."

He looked back at her levelly. "We're still friends, Luisa. You know we are."

She seemed to weigh the truth in his words. Finally, she nodded. "Okay, then. Prove it. Come with Abilene to my cantina next Friday night."

He tried his most forbidding expression. Luisa seemed

completely unaffected by it. And then he demanded, "Will you stop pushing me? I said I would think about it."

"Less thinking, more doing," Luisa advised. She turned to Abilene. "Where are you from?"

"San Antonio."

"A beautiful city. Chula Mesa is not very exciting. It's like many small towns. Not a lot to do, but we have a nice little diner. I like to have my breakfast there on Sundays, after eight o'clock mass. Maybe you would meet me, tomorrow morning at a little after nine? We can get to know each other."

"She doesn't have time for that," Donovan grumbled. "We're on an important project, with a very tight timeline. She works seven days a week."

Abilene ignored him and spoke to Luisa. "I would love that, Luisa. I'll be there."

"Well, then." Luisa's pretty smile bloomed wide. "I'll look forward to seeing you."

They chatted some more, about casual things. And then Luisa got up to leave. Donovan and Abilene followed her to the door.

The minute she was gone, Donovan turned on Abilene. "I'll give you her number. You can call her and tell her you can't make it tomorrow, after all."

Abilene lounged back against the arch that led into the living area. "Why in the world would I want to do that?"

"Because you need to be working. There's no time to waste driving out to the Chula Mesa Diner."

"I can work into the evening some night, if I have to. I'm going, Donovan."

He gave her a long, smoldering look. "What for?"

"I like Luisa. And I can use a little break. I'll be back by eleven, at the latest."

He started to speak again—and then he didn't. Instead, he neatly whirled the chair around and rolled away from her.

Abilene had no trouble finding the diner. It was on Main Street, between Chula Mesa Hardware and Chula Mesa Sunshine Drugs.

She got there before Luisa. She chose a booth with a clear view of the door and ordered coffee for both of them.

Luisa arrived a few minutes later, wearing a snug-fitting V-neck navy blue knit dress and navy blue heels as high as the ones she'd worn the night before. She spotted Abilene immediately and her face lit up with her gorgeous, open smile. "Hey!"

"Hey."

Luisa hurried to join her in the booth. "So you came," she said, leaning across the table, pitching her voice to just above a whisper. "I wasn't sure you would make it."

Abilene frowned. "But I said I would be here."

"You did. But I thought that Donovan would try to change your mind about meeting me alone."

"He did try. But as you can see, my mind is my own."

"Yes, I do see." Luisa said the words approvingly. "But Donovan can be very persuasive, as I'm sure you know."

"Persuasive?" Abilene laughed at that. "No. That's not a word I would use to describe him. He's gruff and exacting. Demanding. Overbearing. Sometimes cruel, though not so much lately. But persuasive? Uh-uh. Not in the least."

"He *used* to be persuasive."

"Yeah? Well, he used to be a lot of things."

Luisa leaned even closer. She reached out, touched the back of Abilene's hand. "He's changed a lot."

"Yeah."

"He must guess that we'll talk about him. He'll hate that."

"Too bad."

The waitress came over. Luisa introduced them. "Margie, this is Abilene…."

When Margie had taken their orders and left them alone, Luisa sipped her coffee and leaned close again. "I do have a few questions. And I'm thinking it will be easier to get the answers from you than from Donovan."

"Ask. Please."

"I heard he had an accident during one of his climbing trips…."

Abilene quickly filled Luisa in on all she knew, from the fall on Dhaulagiri One, to the days alone in the ice cave, to the chain of surgeries. She spoke of his dedication to his physical rehabilitation. And she included what Donovan had told her the morning Ben left—that he *could* walk, though with difficulty, using crutches.

"He seems so sad," said Luisa. At Abilene's nod, she asked, "So what is this project you're working on with him?"

Abilene told her about the children's center, explained that she was the architect who'd won the fellowship he'd offered.

Margie came with the food. She gave them more coffee and left them alone again.

Luisa said, "I remember, a couple of years ago, he

mentioned a plan he had to build a center in San Antonio for children in need. He was passionate about that."

"Well, it's finally happening. We're pulling the design together now. In a few weeks, we'll..." She corrected herself. "*I'll* be going back to SA, to supervise construction."

"He won't go with you? But why not?"

"He says he'll never work again."

"But that's impossible. He loves his work."

"I know. But he says that's all over now."

"He used to travel often, all around the world, building fine hotels, houses for rich people, museums, skyscrapers...."

Abilene set down her slice of toast after only nibbling the crust. "It seems so wrong, I know. He's locked himself up in his house. He won't come out and he won't let anyone in."

"But he let you in."

"I think he finally felt he had to. For the sake of the children who need the center we're building."

"And you've helped him," Luisa said.

"I don't know if I'd go that far."

"Abilene, you let *me* in. And he allowed it."

"Yeah. That's true. He did. Finally."

"You're changing his mind," said Luisa, as if it were such a simple, obvious thing. "You're making him see that life goes on—and life is good. That there's hope and there's meaning. That he can't hide in his house forever, nursing his injuries, feeling sorry for himself. That there's more of life ahead for him, much more. Years and years."

Abilene blew out a breath. "You make it all sound so...possible."

"But of course, it's possible. You're showing him that it is."

"I've been trying, believe me. I don't know *why* I'm trying, exactly. But I am." She fiddled with her napkin, smoothing it on her lap, though it really didn't require smoothing. "I can't...seem to stop myself."

Luisa said simply, "You care for him. There's no shame in that."

She glanced up, met the other woman's waiting eyes. "But I..."

Luisa's smile was soft and knowing. "Yes?"

"Well, I only mean..." She felt suddenly breathless, awkward and tongue-tied. "It's not that we're...intimate. We're not."

Luisa ate a careful bite of her breakfast. "But you do care for him, don't you?"

Abilene sat up straighter. Why should that be so difficult to admit? "Yes, all right. I do. I care for him." A low, confused sound escaped her. "But the way he behaves a lot of the time, I have no idea why."

Luisa laughed. "I know what you mean. Caring for him has to be a very tough job, given the way he is now. But someone's got to do it, got to reach out for him, got to...stick with him, no matter how hard he seems to be pushing everyone away."

"Yeah." Abilene laughed, too, though it came out sounding forced. "I guess I should look at it that way."

"And he is stronger than he knows."

"Oh, Luisa. You think so?"

"I know so. He will come back, to himself, to the world."

"I hope you're right."

"Trust me. I know him. Yes, he suffered a terrible accident. So?" She waved a hand, an airy gesture. "What is all that? What are months of operations and painful rehabilitation? Nothing. Less than nothing, next to losing a child…"

Abilene didn't know what to say. "Luisa, I'm so sorry. I had no idea you'd lost a child."

Luisa pressed her hand against the small gold crucifix at her throat. "Oh, no. Not me."

"But you said—"

"I meant of *his* child. Donovan's child. Elias."

Chapter Six

Abilene could not draw breath.

She felt, suddenly, the same as she had back in the third grade, when the class bully, Billy Trumball, had punched her in the stomach for coming to the defense of a smaller boy. That punch had really knocked the wind out of her. It was an awful, scary feeling, to fear her breath would never come, to gape for air like a landed fish.

She pressed her hand to her stomach, hard. And all at once the air rushed in again. She managed to whisper, "I didn't know…."

Luisa seemed shocked. "He never told you?"

Abilene shook her head. "I know I said we weren't intimate. But even that's an exaggeration. We are so much less than intimate. We're not friends, not even close. I find that I want to understand him, you know? But he's not an easy man to understand. And Ben—Donovan's assistant?"

"Oh, yes. I remember Ben."

"Actually, he quit last Monday, which is another story altogether. But what I'm getting at is that Ben and I, well, I thought we got along. We talked some, about Donovan. About what had happened to make him retreat from the world. I guess I thought I knew more than I did."

"Ben never told you…?"

"Not a word. And Donovan never so much as hinted at such a thing." She leaned across the table, pitched her voice to a whisper. "I just can't believe I never knew. Donovan's a famous man—I mean, to another architect, like me, he's pretty much a living legend. You'd think I would have heard from someone, at some point, that there was a child. And then there's Dax…."

"Dax? I don't know him."

"Dax Girard, my new brother-in-law. He and my baby sister got married a few weeks ago. Dax *knows* Donovan. Not really well, I don't think. But still. Dax never said anything about a lost child."

"Maybe it never came up," Luisa suggested gently. "Elias has been gone for a while now."

"How long?"

"About five years."

"But Luisa, there are no pictures of a child in the house—none that I've seen, anyway."

"No pictures…" Twin lines formed between Luisa's dark brows. "But there were pictures a year ago. One on the piano, of Elias at the beach in California, holding a starfish, smiling his wide, happy smile. One over the fireplace, a large portrait from when he was two or three, in the front room…" Her frown deepened. "I didn't look, last night, when we went through there on the way to the dining room. I didn't notice if Elias's picture was still above the fireplace. And I didn't go into the music room."

"No pictures," Abilene repeated. "Not in the public rooms of the house, anyway. How old was the child—Elias—when he died?"

"Six, I think."

"So you're saying Donovan was married, then?"

Luisa was shaking her head. "Abilene..."

"I just, well, I had no idea he'd been married."

"Please, Abilene."

She sat back in her chair. "What's the matter?"

"I can't say any more."

"But I was hoping, if you could just explain to me—"

"I can't. It's not right." Luisa reached across the table, caught Abilene's hand and held on. Her dark eyes were tender, her expression firm. "I've said too much already. You know I have. The rest is Donovan's to tell."

Donovan went to the studio at a little after ten.

Abilene was still in Chula Mesa with Luisa, wasting the valuable morning hours when she should have been working. He wondered what the two of them were talking about—and then he told himself to stop wondering.

It didn't matter, he tried to convince himself. Whatever they found to chatter about, it had nothing to do with him.

He reviewed, for the second time, the work Abilene had done the day before. He made notes on her progress, notes on what she ought to get accomplished that day. And also notes on what she should be tackling in the next week. She was doing well, was actually a little ahead of where he'd hoped she might be at this time.

The truth was that she continued to thoroughly impress him, with how quickly she learned, with her dedication to the work. In fact, she could probably afford a Sunday morning at the Chula Mesa Diner with Luisa.

Not that he would ever admit that to her face.

She came in at ten forty-five. He felt a rising apprehension at the sight of her, in narrow gray slacks, a coral-colored checked shirt and a jacket nipped in at the waist. Her hair was windblown, her cheeks a healthy pink. He wanted to ask her if she'd had a nice time with Luisa.

But that would have been too friendly. He tried to be careful, not to get friendly with her.

Plus, he really didn't want to know about her breakfast with Luisa. He had a strong intuition that his name had probably come up. Maybe more than once. And he just didn't want to hear what those two might have said about him.

"Ready to work?" He rolled toward her.

She nodded, but didn't say anything as she slipped in behind the drafting table.

He circled the table and glided in beside her. That close, he could smell the light, tempting perfume she wore. She reached up, smoothed her hair. He found himself staring at the silky flesh of her neck, at the pure line of her jaw.

She slid him a look, frowned. "What is it?"

He cleared his throat. "I have notes, a lot of them."

"Well, all right then." Her voice sounded…what? Careful? Breathless? He wasn't sure. She added, "Let's get started."

He had dual urges—both insane. To ask her if everything was all right. To run the back of his finger down the satin skin of her neck, and to feel for the first time with conscious intent, the texture of her flesh.

Seriously. Was he losing his mind?

They went to work.

An hour later, he left her to continue on her own. He checked on her at three, then changed into sweats and went down to the gym where he worked out on his own, a long session with the free weights and then another, equally long, of simple walking, back and forth, with the aid of the parallel bars, sweating bullets with each step.

His legs really were getting stronger. Recently, he'd found he was capable of standing long enough to make use of a urinal, even without a nearby wall or a bar to brace himself with. It was milestone of which he was inordinately proud.

At five, he returned to the main floor. He dropped in on her again before he went to clean up, because it was getting late and he was afraid she'd have left the studio if he took the time to shower first.

She was still there. "Just getting ready to wrap things up for the day," she told him. That green-golden gaze ran over him. "Good workout?"

"Yes, it was." He felt sweaty and grungy, and he probably smelled like a hard-ridden horse. But he should have thought of that before he came wheeling in here without a shower. "Let's see how you're doing…."

She showed him what she'd come up with in the past hour and a half. They briefly discussed what was going well. And what wasn't quite coming together.

They agreed that they had a good handle on the arrangement of space now. But they'd also decided the design had to speak of fun, of possibility. Probably of flight. That, they had begun to think, was the eventual *parti:* early flight.

Somehow, they needed to get the theme of flight into the facade and the main entry, so that when parents and children and teachers came to the center every day they felt a sense of uplift, that anything could happen in this special place, that they, the children who grew and learned there, could do anything they set their young minds to accomplishing.

This was the central idea for the structure. And that meant they needed to get a serious grip on it soon, since the rest of the complex would be likely to change, once they found the true heart of the project.

"Soon," he said, affirming what they both knew needed to happen. "I know you're going to find it soon."

She was straightening her workspace by then. "Well, probably not tonight. Right now, I think I could use a long, hard swim."

He had a sudden, stunning vision of her, emerging from the courtyard pool, all wet and gleaming, the water sliding off her body in glittering streams.

"Uh. Yeah," he said stupidly. "A swim. Good idea. Clear your head."

She regarded him. It was a strange, piercing sort of look. He almost wondered if she could see inside his mind, if she knew that he had watched her, in her blue tank suit, out in the courtyard, when she thought she was alone.

Well, if she did suspect him of spying on her, she could stop worrying. He would never do such a thing again.

"See you at dinner," she said, still eyeing him in that odd way—or at least, so it seemed to him.

"Yes," he answered distractedly. "See you at dinner."

And she left him.

He made himself stay behind in the studio, which was one of the few main floor areas without a view of the courtyard—and the pool. He went to his desk and he pushed his computer monitors out of the way, and he spent an hour sketching, plugging away at the facade problem.

At six-thirty, no closer to any kind of solution than he had been when he started, he went back to his own rooms to shower before dinner.

The lights in the courtyard were on by then. And before he turned on any lights in his sitting room, he went to the glass doors and gazed out.

The pool was deserted—which he had known it would be.

And he felt disappointed, that she wasn't still out there, after all—a feeling he knew to be completely reprehensible.

He whirled and rolled through his bedroom, and the wide-open double doors to the bathroom, where he tore off his sweats and used the railings he'd had installed months ago, to get into the open shower and onto the bathing stool waiting there.

Twenty minutes later, he was clean and dressed and on his way to the dining room.

Abilene was already there, in a simple long-sleeve black dress, standing at the doors that looked out on the courtyard. She turned when he entered.

In her eyes, he thought he saw questions. His guard went up.

But then she smiled. And all she said was, "There you are." Now she seemed almost happy to see him.

And he was glad, absurdly glad. That she hadn't asked any questions. That she had smiled.

They went to the small table that Olga had set for them. He wished he could stand up, step close to her, pull back her chair. Such a simple gesture, but not something he could do. Not yet, anyway.

And possibly, not ever.

She sat. He wheeled around the table and took the waiting place across from her. Olga had lit the candles, and already served the soup. And the wine was there, opened.

He poured. For Abilene. And then for him. He raised his glass. She touched hers to it. They sipped. Shared a nod.

Ate the soup.

Olga appeared with the salads. She took their empty bowls away, refilled their wineglasses. And vanished again.

They ate the salad, sipped more wine.

The whole dinner was like that. He didn't talk. Neither did Abilene.

But he felt…together with her, somehow. In collusion. Connected.

And that made him wonder, as he had more than once that day, if he might really be losing his mind somehow, slipping over the edge into some strange self-delusion.

On the mountain, in the snow cave, alone with his pain, he'd known he was going mad. He was crazy. And he was going to die.

On the mountain, he understood everything. He talked to Elias.

He was ready to go.

And there had been peace in that, a kind of completion.

When they dragged him back to the world, peace became the thing that eluded him.

Until tonight, for some unknown reason. Tonight, in the quiet of the dining room. Sharing a meal with Abilene.

It ended too soon. She got up, smiled again at him, said good-night.

"Good night," he answered, and watched her go.

The room seemed empty without her. Yet another sign of his current slide into total insanity.

Tomorrow, he promised himself, in the bright light of morning, the world would right itself. He would be the man he had become in the past year. Self-contained. Wanting no one. Needing no one.

Alone.

In her rooms, Abilene changed into the old pair of sweats and worn T-shirt she usually slept in. She brushed her teeth. And then she paced the floor for a while.

What had just happened, in the dining room?

She had questions for Donovan. And she'd fully intended to ask them. She had planned to be delicate about it. And respectful. But really, there was so much she wanted to know.

And she'd accepted that Luisa was right. If she wanted answers—about whether Donovan had been married, about his wife, if there had been one, about the child he had lost—well, it was only fair that she ask the man himself.

But then she'd turned from the doors to the courtyard to find him sitting there, so gorgeous, so self-contained, so guarded….

And she couldn't do it. She didn't even *want* to do it, to pry into his mind and his secret heart. To ferret out the answers he didn't want to share.

All she wanted was to be with him.

Simply. Gracefully. For an evening.

To share a meal with him, if not as a friend, at least as a temporary companion, a guest in his house. She was grateful to him, she realized, for teaching her so much, for guiding her at the same time as he prodded her forward. For demanding so much of her, for never letting her off easy.

For being such a fascinating man.

So she had done exactly what she wanted. She'd shared a quiet meal with him.

And now she paced her sitting room, feeling edgy and full of nervous energy, not understanding herself any better than she understood him.

Eventually, she gave up wearing a path into the hardwood floor. She got out her cell and called home, called her mom, and her sister, Zoe, who was just back from her honeymoon.

Yes, she was tempted to ask Zoe if she would speak with Dax, try to find out from him if he knew that Donovan had had a son. But she didn't. She reminded herself that Donovan was the one she should ask about the child.

If she ever asked anyone at all.

She called Javier to see how things were going with him—and then ended up going on and on about the design for the children's center, about the idea for the facade that still wasn't coming together, about how much she was learning from Donovan. As always, he encouraged her and he asked all the right questions.

By the time she hung up with Javier, it was after ten. She got into bed and turned off the light and told herself that she was glad she'd decided not to hound Donovan anymore about his past, about his secrets, about his private life.

From now on, she would do the job she had come here to do, period. She would be pleasant at dinner, in a thoroughly surface sort of way. And in three weeks, she would leave this house and the solitary man who lived here. She would build a special children's center and get a great job with a top firm.

And if she ever thought of Donovan McCrae again, it would be with simple gratitude for the opportunity he had given her.

Donovan woke at ten after six Monday morning with the facade, vestibule and welcome area of the children's center clear in his mind.

He could see it. He understood it. He knew how to build it. He *had it,* damn it.

He knew how it should be.

He needed to draw it, fast. And then he needed for Abilene to see it. He couldn't wait to show it to her. This was the breakthrough they'd been waiting for.

After today, it was all going to fall into place. And fast. Even faster than it had up till now.

He sat bolt-upright in bed, threw back the covers and swung his legs to the side, unthinking. His feet hit the floor and he leaned forward to stand.

The arrows of shimmering pain brought him up short. He looked down at the deep grooves of scar tissue, scoring his thighs, the flesh over his knees, which were now made of metal and plastic, and lower, to his skinny, wasted calves.

He tossed back his head and laughed out loud.

It was the first time since the fall down the mountain that he'd actually forgotten there was a problem with his legs.

After that, he took it a little slower. But not a lot. He was a man with a mission, and the mission was to get the concept in his head down onto paper, to take what he'd discovered and to show it to Abilene.

What he'd discovered. Sometimes an inspired design

element felt like that: like a discovery. Not as if he'd created it at all. But as if it had been waiting, whole and ready, for him to finally see it.

He rang Olga and asked her to bring him coffee in the studio. And then he threw on some clothes and wheeled at breakneck speed out of his rooms and down the hall.

In the studio, he turned on some lights to boost what natural light there was from the skylights and the clerestory windows, so early on a gray winter morning. He got out large sheets of drawing paper and soft pencils and he went to work.

It came so fast, he could barely keep up with it, his hand moving, utterly sure, across the paper, every stroke exactly right, no hesitation. Just a direct channel to the idea that was waiting, so impatiently now, to reveal itself.

When he finished, he looked over and saw that Olga had come and gone, leaving the coffee he'd asked for, along with a couple of Anton's killer cinnamon rolls. He took time for a cup, ate half a cinnamon roll.

By then, it was after seven. And there was no way he could wait any longer. Even if Abilene came to the studio early, it could still be an hour before she put in an appearance. Before he could show her what he had.

He couldn't do it, wait that long.

So he gathered the drawings—the one of the facade, the one of the entry interior and the one from the floor of the welcome area, looking up. He rolled them, snapped a band around them, laid them across his thighs and went to find her.

Often she would grab breakfast in the kitchen, so he wheeled there first and stuck his head in. Anton stood at the stove stirring something that made his stomach growl.

"Abilene?" Donovan asked.

"Haven't seen her yet today."

"Thanks." And he was off down the interior hallway.

He reached the door to her sitting room and braked sideways to it, gave it a strong tap, called, "Abilene?"

She didn't answer.

He knocked again.

Nothing.

Was she still in bed? If so, she needed to get up. Now. She needed to see this and she needed to get herself together and get to work.

He tried the doorknob. It turned.

So he pushed the door inward. "Abilene?"

Still no answer. She must be a sound sleeper.

Too bad. It was imperative that he get her up, that he share with her what he'd found out. She was going to be so happy, so relieved. It was all coming together, and it would be a really fine piece of work, something they could both be proud of.

He wheeled over the threshold and into her private space. The bedroom door, in the far corner to the left as he entered, was wide open, so he went for it, rolling the length of the sitting room and then into her bedroom.

The blinds were drawn against the morning light, the bed unmade. And empty. The bathroom door, directly across from the door to the sitting room, stood open. The light was on in there. And he could hear the unmistakable sound of the shower running, feel the moisture in the air…

He backed and turned, approaching the bed. He saw the black dress she'd worn the night before, laid across the bedside chair. Saw her cell phone on the nightstand, beside a half-full glass of water, and a framed snapshot of a bunch of good-looking, smiling people. He picked it up, that picture, for a closer look.

Her family. They stood out in the country somewhere, in front of a weathered cabin. Father and mother. Seven broad-shouldered brothers. Abilene—but younger, her face a little rounder than now. And another girl who resembled her.

Carefully, he set the picture back exactly where he'd found it.

He knew where she had to be, of course. Had known when he saw the light from the bathroom, heard the sound of the water running in there. He knew he should wheel around, roll into the sitting room, and on out the way he had come.

But he didn't wheel away. All he could think was that she had to see what he had to show her.

He backed up, turned his wheels toward the sound of running water, and rolled on through that open bathroom door.

Chapter Seven

She was in there, as he had known she would be.

In the shower. The doorless, open shower.

Wearing nothing but the slim, smooth perfection of her own skin, facing away from him, her head tipped up to the shower spray, eyes closed, soap and water sheeting down over her pink-tipped breasts, her concave belly, her gently curving hips, her perfect bottom, her long, lean thighs.

He stopped the chair without a sound.

And he watched as she turned her body in a gentle, side to side swaying motion, rinsing herself, letting the spray carry the bubbles away. He saw her from the back, and then in profile, and then full front.

At first, it was the same as when he watched her in the pool. A pure appreciation of something so beautiful, so smooth—her skin flushed, steamy; the secret shadow beneath her arm as she slicked her wet hair back. The soft, round curve of the side of her breast.

But in seconds, everything changed. It became more than just about the perfect picture she made, more than the slim, womanly shape of her, more than the frothy dribble of bubbles sliding down sleek, youthful skin.

He saw her as a woman.

Desirable to him.

More than desirable.

Wanted. Yearned for. Craved.

The reality of the situation became all at once blindingly clear. He had been lying—to her, and more than to her, to himself. He'd treated her callously, cruelly.

Because she stirred him. She…excited him. From their initial meeting, in the studio, when Ben brought her to him on that first day, he had felt it—the brisk wind of change on the air.

Felt a sense of possibility, of promise. As if she had marched into a darkened, stuffy room on those long, strong legs of hers, run up the shut blinds, and thrown the windows wide.

He'd been blinking and whining and sniping against the light ever since. Like some cranky old man.

Yes. Like an old man. An old man awakened abruptly from a long, fitful sleep. He'd been digging at her, taunting her, trying to get her to give up and go, to leave him in peace—but at the same time he couldn't help but be drawn to her.

She was not only a joy to look at, she had an incisive intelligence. She questioned everything, wanted to see beneath the surface, to understand the deeper truth. And beyond looks and brains, she possessed a kind and generous heart.

She was pretty much perfect. His ideal woman.

And he had met her too late.

All this came to him in an instant—the instant before she turned beneath the spray and opened her eyes.

She let out a shriek, blinked fiercely against the water that still ran into her eyes, blinding her—and looked again. "Donovan? What in the...?" She turned, twisted the knob to cut off the water, at the same time as she groped for the towel on the rack outside the shower stall.

He spun the chair to face the door, giving her the chance to cover herself, at least. And then he just sat there, the rolled drawings he'd *had* to show her waiting in his lap, feeling not only reprehensible, but shamed beyond bearing.

Was she wrapped in a towel yet? She was absolutely silent behind him. All he heard were the final hollow drip-drip-drips of water on slate from the shut-off shower heads.

And he couldn't think of a damn thing to say. Sorry was not going to cut it. And as for trying to justify what he'd just done? There was no justification. None.

She spoke then, her voice low and tight. "Would you just leave, please?"

It was the permission he'd been waiting for. She had released him. He didn't look back at her. He kept his gaze straight ahead as he wheeled out of the bathroom, across the dim bedroom, down the empty sitting room and out through the open hallway door.

Abilene's first thought, once she heard him shut the outer door behind him, was that she needed to go. She needed to get her stuff packed, throw it in her car and get out, go home, back to San Antonio where she belonged.

Really, she couldn't stay here anymore. She just couldn't.

She traded the hastily grabbed towel for the robe that hung on the back of the bathroom door. Her hair hung in snaky coils, still dripping wet, and she left a trail of droplets across the bedroom floor as she pulled back the door to the walk-in closet, went in there and grabbed an empty suitcase, the largest one of the three she had brought with her.

She hauled it back into the bedroom, tossed it on the bed, got hold of the zipper tab and ripped it along the track until she had it undone. Then she flipped the top back, spreading it wide.

After that, she just stood there, staring into the empty space within, still dripping on the bedside rug, feeling overwhelmed and awful and foolish.

And also numb, somehow.

She shook herself. Then she turned on her bare heel and marched back into the closet, where she grabbed a bunch of stuff, hangers and all, and lugged it back to the open suitcase. When she got there, she flung the whole pile into the yawning interior.

Bracing her hands on her hips, she stared down at the tangle of shirts and light jackets, knit tops and cardigan sweaters.

"What a mess," she whispered, to no one in particular. "What a stupid, crazy mess."

She turned, sank to the edge of the bed and gazed blindly toward the open door to the closet and thought how, if she was going to go, she shouldn't be just sitting here, staring off into space. She needed to finish packing, to put on some clothes, to dry her hair.

But she didn't get up. She continued to sit there. By then, she was thinking that she didn't really want to go.

She wanted to finish the design for the children's center. She wanted her chance to see it built.

And still, the yearning remained within her, to understand what was going on with Donovan, to…talk to him, or *not* to talk. Just to be with him the way they had been at dinner the night before. To enjoy spending time with him. Without having to be constantly on guard against his sudden, inexplicable cruelty.

She wanted to be able to laugh with him, to speak openly. Honestly. Without fear of emotional ambush or petty retaliation.

With a heavy sigh, she got up, scooped the tangle of clothing and hangers into her arms, carried them back to the closet, and hung them up again. She returned to the bedroom, shut the suitcase, zipped it tight and put it away.

She was just emerging from the closet when she heard the polite tap on the sitting room door.

What now?

"It's open," she called, and then went over and sat on the long, rustic bench at the end of the bed.

She heard the outer door open. A moment later, Donovan appeared in the bedroom doorway.

He stopped the chair there, hands tight on the wheels, and waited, his fine mouth a grim line, his eyes bleak.

She was still naked under the robe and her hair hung on her shoulders in wet clumps. But so what? He'd already seen everything anyway.

Carefully, she smoothed the robe on her bare knees. Then she drew her shoulders back and aimed her chin high. "You have something you want to say?"

He nodded. And then, finally, with obvious difficulty, he said, "An apology seems ridiculous. It's not as though I have any excuse for my behavior."

She said nothing. If he had some kind of explanation to make, well, let him go for it.

He didn't waver, didn't look away. "Ridiculous," he repeated. "But nonetheless necessary." His eyes were dark right then, haunted. Gunmetal gray. He drew in a slow breath. "And so I do, I apologize. For what that's worth, which I know is not a lot."

She fiddled with the tie of the robe, nervously. And realized the action betrayed her. So she let it go and wrapped her arms tightly around her middle. "These rooms are the one thing I have here, for myself, in this house. The one place I don't have to be on guard, ever. The one place you are not allowed to be."

"You're right. I know." He let out another careful, pained breath and lowered his golden head. In shame, she hoped.

Because he *should* be ashamed.

She accused, "And now you've not only invaded my space, you've wheeled on into my bathroom and watched me in the shower." She waited until he lifted his head and met her eyes. And then she gave him a look meant to sear him where he sat. "I turned around and you were… just sitting there, watching me. Why?"

"There's no excuse," he muttered low.

"No argument there. I'll ask you again. Why?"

It took him a long count of five to answer. "Because you're beautiful—or at least, at first, that was why."

She scoffed, "What? I should be flattered now?"

"No. Of course not. I'm just trying to explain myself. Not that anything I say is going to make it okay. But you should know that at first, it was a totally objective appreciation."

"Objective?" She let out a harsh laugh. "As in detached?"

"I suppose so."

"And is that supposed to ease my mind somehow? That you broke into my rooms, rolled into my bathroom and looked at me—*stared* at me without my clothes on—and you felt nothing?"

"I didn't say I felt nothing—I said I saw you...I don't know, without heat, I guess."

What was he telling her? She had no idea. She should leave it alone, send him away.

But she didn't. "You looked at me coolly? Dispassionately. Is that it?"

"No. There was passion. But it wasn't personal. It was more the way I would admire good art."

"Good art." She shook her head. "I have to tell you, Donovan. This is one strange conversation."

He wheeled a fraction closer—caught himself, and wheeled back to where he'd been before. "There's more. You should know the rest of it. There should be honesty between us, at least."

Honesty. Well, okay. She agreed with him about the honesty. She *wanted* honesty.

She wanted that a lot.

"What else then?" She looked at him sideways, needing the truth, yes. But contrarily, not really sure she wanted to know whatever he might reveal next.

He revealed it anyway. "I watched you swimming, too."

Her cheeks were suddenly burning. She pressed her palms to them. "Oh, great. And I need to know that, why?"

"Because it's the truth. It's what I did. And I don't want to lie to you, by omission or otherwise, about what I did. I owe you that much, at least."

She had no idea how to answer that. So she simply sat there, waiting, for whatever he would say next.

He went on, "And it was the same, when I watched you swimming, as it was at first a little while ago, in there." He gestured toward the bathroom. "There was appreciation. Admiration. A vague, faraway sense of longing, I guess you could say."

She sat forward, curious in spite of herself. "Longing for...?"

"I don't know. For the man I was once. For the past. For the present and the future, too. But not as they are and will be. As they *might* have been."

She thought of his child then, of the little boy. His lost son, Elias. She longed to ask him about Elias.

But no. Bringing up Elias now would only send them spinning off in another direction entirely. They needed, right now, to stay with the subject at hand.

The painful, awkward, weird—and thoroughly embarrassing—subject at hand.

She raked her fingers back through her soggy hair. "So. You felt appreciation. Objective appreciation."

"Yes. When I watched you swimming. And today, too. At first. But then it changed."

Her throat clutched. She gulped hard, to make it relax. "Changed?"

"That's right. It became...something more. I found I was attracted. To you. As a man is attracted to a woman. It stopped being objective. I realized I want you. And I haven't wanted anything or anyone since before the accident on the mountain—a long time before."

I want you. Had he actually just said that out loud?

Okay, she truly was not ready to be having this conversation. Maybe she would never be ready. To speak of desire, of attraction, of *sex* with Donovan McRae.

That wasn't why she'd come here, worked her butt off, put up with his antagonism and his ruthless remarks. She was here for the work, and only the work. She had absolutely no interest in…

She caught herself up short.

Who was she kidding?

She did have an interest in Donovan, as a man. She had a serious interest.

He had captivated her from the beginning. From the first time she saw him, as a dewy-eyed undergraduate, one in hundreds in the audience on that long-ago evening when he came to speak at Rice.

And since she'd been here, in his house, it was pretty much a toss-up over which fascinated her more: the work she'd come out here to do, or the man in the wheelchair across the bedroom from her.

In the end, it was pretty simple. Much simpler than either of them were allowing it to be. She wanted him. And he wanted her.

They should start with that. See where it led them…

But really, *how* to start? *That* was not simple. Not with a man like Donovan.

She rose and walked past him, crossing to the French doors. She opened the blinds. The winter sunlight spilled in, filling the room, gray and cool. Outside, the wind found its way into the courtyard, ruffled just slightly the glassy surface of the pool.

He said her name, "Abilene."

She turned to look at him again.

His gaze didn't waver. He sat absolutely still at the threshold of her bedroom, waiting.

She asked, "But why?"

"Why, what?"

"Why did you come in here in the first place? I mean, it's one thing to look out a window and see me in the pool. It's another to wheel right into my bathroom when you can hear the shower running and have to be reasonably certain you'll find me stark naked in there."

He lifted one shoulder in a halfhearted shrug. In the morning light, she could see he hadn't shaved yet. Golden stubble shone on his lean cheeks and sculpted jaw. He said, "I told you, there's no excuse."

"You're right. There isn't." But there had to be something. "But I think there *is* a reason, isn't there?"

He blew out a breath. "Fine. Yeah. There's a reason." He didn't say what—really, the man was beyond exasperating.

She was forced to prompt him again. "Okay. *What* reason?"

And he finally gave it up. "I figured out the answer to our main problem. You must know how it is, when the solution finally comes." He held out both hands to the side, palms up. "Magic time. I woke up this morning and I knew what we had to do…."

"Wait a minute…" She felt suddenly breathless. Buoyant. "You mean you figured out what we need for the entry and the facade?"

He nodded.

"Oh, Donovan. That's huge."

He lowered his head and spoke with real modesty. "It seemed that way at the time."

"I can't believe it. This is fabulous. So you, what? You dreamed it?"

"Well, I wouldn't say that, exactly. I just woke up and I knew. I went to the studio. I couldn't get it down fast enough. And when I had it, I came looking for you. I couldn't wait to show you. It seemed important at the time."

"Donovan. It *is* important. It's everything—I mean, *if* you've really got it…."

"Oh, I've got it." A slow smile burst across his wonderful face. He looked so charming, when he smiled.

She remembered then. When she had turned in the shower and opened her eyes, saw him sitting there, big as life in her bathroom: there had been rolled drawings in his lap. "You had them with you before, didn't you?"

"Yeah."

"But where are they now?"

"I went back to the studio. I left them in there."

"Why didn't you tell me that up front? I mean, it would have made what you did a little easier to understand."

"I told you. That would have been an excuse. And there is no excuse." He glanced away, then back at her again. "Do you…want to see them?"

"Are you kidding? I can't wait to see them."

"You're not leaving, then?" He looked so hopeful, his face open and eager.

And she saw, at that moment, the man he had been, the man she had glimpsed from a distance once so long ago, before he lost a child. Before he fell down a mountain. Before all the things that can kill a man inside, make him hard and cold, cruel at heart.

"No," she said. "I'm not leaving."

Already, he was backing, clearing the doorway so he could turn. "Then get dressed. Meet me in the studio…."

"Donovan." She said his name softly. But it was, unmistakably, a command.

He froze, his strong body drawn taut, rigid in the chair.

She said, slowly and deliberately, "Stay. Please. Stay here with me. Just for a little while, all right?"

He stared, perhaps sensing the direction of her thoughts, yet not really believing. And then he whispered, "But I don't..." For once, he didn't have the words.

She asked, gently now, "Would you come out of the doorway, please? Would you...come here?"

He started to come to her—then stopped the chair with a firm grip on the wheels. "Abilene..."

"Hmm?"

"You really don't want to go there."

"Don't tell me what I want. You'll get it wrong every time."

His dark gold lashes swept down, then instantly lifted again to reveal watchful, stricken eyes. "I only mean, it's not a good idea. We've cleared the air between us. You've decided to stay, to finish what we started. Now we can forget about all this."

"Forget?" It hurt, a lot, that he had decided to make what had passed between them just now sound so unimportant, so trivial. "Would it be that easy for you, to pretend this morning never happened?"

"You know what I mean. We can go forward, do the work that has to be done, leave the rest of it alone."

"The rest of it?"

He glanced beyond her, toward the open bathroom door. The light was still on in there. She followed his gaze briefly, long enough to see what he saw—the gleaming trail of water across the floor. Her towel in a damp clump, right where she had dropped it when she grabbed for her robe.

"It would only lead to trouble," he said gruffly, at

last, still looking past her. "I'm no good for that, not anymore."

She made herself ask, "No good for what?"

He shut his eyes again. And that time, when he opened them, he met her gaze with defiance. And such stark, determined loneliness. "No good for any of it. Sex. Love. A future with someone—with you."

She tried for a teasing note. "Love and the future, huh? Well, Donovan, we really don't have to tackle everything at once."

He laughed, as she'd hoped he might. But it was a gruff laugh, a sound with more pain than humor in it.

"And as for sex…" She was looking down again, at her own bare feet on the hardwood floor. She drew her head up to find him watching her, his focus absolute. Unwavering. Waiting for her to finish what she'd so boldly begun. She blurted out, "Well, does it work? I mean, *can* you…? Is there some kind of damage, or is it all in your mind?"

A silence from him. Then, warily, "How many questions was that? Four?"

She was not backing off on this. "So pick one."

He did, after a moment. "There's no physical problem."

"So it's a psychological issue, then?"

"Abilene." He said her name in a weary voice. "Psychological. Emotional. Mental. I have no clue, okay? In the past year, I never so much as thought about it. It wasn't as if I cared."

"Oh." Disappointment had her shoulders drooping. She whispered, "I see…"

"At least, not until about twenty-five minutes ago." Was that an actual gleam she now saw in his eyes?

"Oh!" She snapped up straight again. Of course. How

could she have forgotten? He'd already said it—that he wanted her, in a man/woman way. "So you *can*, then? You're…able?"

"Yeah. I'm able."

She found she was grinning. And then he was grinning, too.

And then they were both laughing, together.

It felt so good, to laugh with him. As good as she'd dared to imagine it might. She wanted to go to him, to touch him, to lay her hand against his beard-stubbled cheek, maybe bend down and press her lips to his.

But he had stopped laughing. He was watching her again. And his eyes were wary.

So she didn't approach him. She went past him, to the side of the bed, and sat down. The silence stretched out. Finally, she couldn't bear it any longer. "Well, okay. I'm relieved—not that we couldn't have worked something out. I mean, there are a lot of different ways to make love."

He said nothing to that, only arched a gold-dusted brow.

What? Had she said something that offended him? She felt breathless all over again. And embarrassed, too. But still, she refused to give up on this.

She suggested what she hadn't quite had the nerve to do. "Maybe just a kiss. Would that be all right? We could start with a kiss. For now."

He stayed where he was, in the doorway. And he asked, so gently, "Is that wise?"

"Oh, come on." She threw up both hands. "What do you mean, wise? Is a kiss ever wise? What kind of question is that?"

"You just need to be aware that I meant what I said."

"About…?"

"Love. A future for you and me, together. It's not going to happen. You would have to understand that, going in."

She realized she could easily become irritated with him again—she *was* irritated with him again. "A minute ago, you said there couldn't be sex, either. But it seems to me that already, you've changed your mind about sex."

He only nodded. Slowly. "I'm a man. Men are weak. On two legs—or on wheels."

She wasn't buying that lame excuse. "You're not weak. We both know that. Blind and stubborn and needlessly cruel, maybe. But weak? Never."

He held his ground—in the doorway, as well as in his intractable, impossible attitude. "You should think it over. Better yet, you should forget the whole thing."

She pressed her palms to the tangled sheets, braced forward on them. And tried, one more time, to get through to him, to get them back to the way it had been between them such a short time before. "Is that what you want, seriously? To forget this morning? Forget what happened? Forget everything that we said?"

He frowned. And then he said her name, so softly, with tender feeling, "Abilene…"

And for a split second, she *believed.*

She believed in him, in the possible future. In the hope of love. She was certain he would at least admit that there was no way he could forget what had passed between them just now.

For that beautiful instant, she could see it, all of it, just as it would go. See him shaking his head as he confessed that no, he couldn't forget, didn't *want* to forget. And then she could see herself rising, going to him, bending close to him, claiming his mouth in their first lovely, tender, exploratory kiss.

But then he said, “Yes. It’s what I want. I think that forgetting would be for the best.”

Chapter Eight

And that was it. It was over between them—over without ever really getting started.

He backed, turned, glanced over his shoulder. "The studio, then?"

She nodded, pressed her lips together, made them relax. "I'll be there soon."

He left her rooms for the second time that morning, again shutting the door to the main hall quietly behind him.

"Ho-kay," she said aloud to the silent bedroom, once he was gone. "So we forget."

She rose, went to the bathroom, hung up her towel, dried her hair, brushed on mascara, applied a little blusher and some lip gloss. She took off her robe, hung it on the door, rolled on deodorant, spritzed on scent.

Back in the bedroom, she got dressed.

Her stomach was empty and she needed her morning

shot of caffeine, so she stopped in at the kitchen to grab something to eat. Anton gave her a big mug of fragrant, fresh-brewed coffee and told her that Donovan had already ordered breakfast for her. It was waiting in the studio.

She wanted to snap at Anton, to inform him in no uncertain terms that Donovan didn't get to decide everything, that where she ate her breakfast damn well ought to be up to her.

But it wasn't Anton's fault that she felt like biting someone's head off. She thanked him and went on her way.

In the studio, Donovan was at his desk. He glanced up when she entered.

She gave him a nod—one minus eye contact—and followed her nose to the credenza where Olga had left the food. Under the warming lid were light-as-air scrambled eggs, and the raisin toast she adored. She grabbed the plate and a fork and carried them and her coffee back to her work area, where she ate. Slowly. Savoring every bite.

Donovan didn't say a word. Not until she'd carried the empty plate back to the credenza and helped herself to more coffee from the carafe waiting there. She had no idea what he was doing while she was eating. She was very careful not to glance his way.

Not even once.

But the moment she set the plate back on the credenza, he said, "Come here. Have a look."

A sharp retort rose to her lips. She bit it back. *Forget,* she reminded herself. *We are forgetting....*

She went to him, circling around the giant desk, until she stood at his elbow. The drawings were spread out in front of him.

For a moment, she refused to look down. She sipped her coffee. She gazed in the general direction of the door she had entered through, thinking how she almost wished she could go out that door and keep walking.

Never come back.

"Abilene." He had tipped his head back, was looking at her.

She went ahead and did it, let herself look at *him.*

Zap. Like a bolt of lightning in the desert, visible for miles. Heat flared across her skin.

How stupid and pointless, to feel this way.

It had been better when she had been in denial about it.

Forgetting, she reminded herself. Again. *We are forgetting.*

She tore her gaze from his and turned her focus to the sketches.

And instantly, she felt better. Her injured fury faded to nothing. Because she had something else to think about. Something important.

Something that mattered as much—no. *More,* she told herself silently. Insistently. *The work matters more than whatever is never going to happen between this impossible, exasperating man and me.*

She leaned closer.

How had he done it? It was perfect. It was exactly right—a series of wide, overlapping skylit arches high above the entrance, like the wings of transparent birds, spread in flight. From the front, it almost seemed that the building itself was about to take to the air.

And from inside, in the entry and welcome area, the arches were wings, too, but now, wings seen from below, wings three stories up, wings spread wide, wings already claiming the endless sky.

She said, "Oh, Donovan, exactly. It's exactly right. Astonishing. Perfect."

"You think?" He sounded young again. Hopeful. Proud.

"I *know,*" she told him. "It's what we've been needing, what we've been waiting for."

And she really did feel better about everything then.

After all, hadn't he said at the beginning that he would never work again?

And yet he *was* working.

The proof of that was spread on the big desk before her. He was working. He was changing. No matter how hard he tried to deny his own awakening, he was beginning to care how the whole thing turned out.

What was it Luisa had said? *He will come back, to himself, to the world.*

Abilene could see that now. He was already coming back.

And even if there was never any hope for the two of them, as lovers. Even if there was no future for them, together.

Well, she could live with that. It would be something, at least, to know that she'd helped him a little, that she had contributed to his finding his life and his work again. It would be a fair trade. More than fair—for the chance she was getting, this fellowship that had miraculously become her own project, only better. It had become a cocreation, both hers. And his.

She said, "These wings…"

"Yeah?"

"The image should be everywhere. In the bottom of the pool."

"I like that."

"In the play yards, embossed in the concrete. In the floor of the cafeteria and the multiuse room...." She was already reaching for more drawing paper.

He handed her a soft marker. She began to draw.

It was a good week.

They did fine work. Now that they had the heart of the design down, they found a thousand ways to use it to enrich the rest of the building, so that the center really started to work as a structure with a specific purpose, a place where children who had started out without a lot in life would be free to learn and to grow, to reach for the sky.

They also had another guest.

Tuesday afternoon, one of Donovan's former climbing partners came to the door. Donovan could have had Olga or Helen, his new assistant, send the visitor away. But he went to answer the doorbell himself.

He even let the guy in. His name was Alan Everson. Alan was long-faced, lean and weather-beaten, a very serious man. He'd driven all the way from Albuquerque to see Donovan.

After dinner, Abilene left the two men alone. They went to the game room, where there was a pool table and a bar and tables for card games, very much like the game room at her family's ranch, Bravo Ridge. It was the first time, as far as Abilene knew, that Donovan had entered the game room since she'd been staying in his house.

She hoped they played pool, or maybe chess. And that they talked about old times, about who was attempting which mountain and when.

Alan left after breakfast Wednesday morning. Abilene asked Donovan if he'd enjoyed the other man's visit.

"Yeah," he said gruffly. "It was good to see him." But

he didn't elaborate. And she didn't push him for details. Really, if he was willing to let his friends come around again, that was enough.

At least for now.

Thursday, in the early morning, just as they started working in the studio, Donovan got a call. Instead of telling Helen to deal with it for him, he took the phone.

Abilene was at her own desk, on the computer there, using the CAD software to get going on the key technical drawings the engineers were going to need. Later, more architects would be hired to produce the endless number of necessary drawings. But she needed to get the basics down—as well as a simple schematic CAD rendering of the center, which had advantages over manual study and presentation models. With computer-assisted drawings, the views could be expanded, manipulated, made to show any aspect of the design from within, below or in aerial views.

Yes, when Donovan answered the buzzing phone on his desk and said, "I'll talk to her, Helen," Abilene could have taken a break, given him a little privacy.

But hey. She was curious. Was it Luisa? And if not, who else, beyond Luisa and Alan, was he willing to speak with, at last?

Her name, as it turned out, was Mariah. And Donovan didn't sound especially happy to hear from her.

His side of the conversation was mostly in the negative. "No, Mariah. I'm fine, Mariah. I'm sorry…. I know. I should have gotten back with you long before now…. No, I can't. I've got a lot to deal with at this point and…" The woman must have really started in on him about then, because he fell silent. He made a few impatient noises. And then he finally said, "Look. I don't think so…." Another silence from him, then, "Take my word for it. Move on. I meant what I said, and I said no." He hung up.

Abilene tried to decide whether to remark on his curtness. Or get back to work.

He made the decision for her by accusing, "I know you were listening."

She peered around the side of her computer screen. "Uh. Well. Yeah. Guilty."

He rolled out from behind his own wall of computers so he could see her while he lectured her. "You're always accusing *me* of being rude. But somehow, the rules are different for you. You could have given me a moment or two alone, to take that call."

"I considered it. But then, well, I was curious, so I stayed."

"You were curious. And that makes it okay to listen in on my private conversations?"

"Donovan. Do you really want to lecture me about respecting *your* privacy?" She gave him her sweetest smile. He glared back at her. But he didn't argue. She said, more gently, "Come on. If it was so private, *you* could have left the room—and I'm guessing that Mariah will not be coming to dinner?"

He stared at her, narrowed-eyed, from across the room. And then he grunted. "No, she won't."

She couldn't resist asking, "An old girlfriend?"

He actually volunteered a little information. "Mariah lives in Dallas. She's a successful interior designer. I met her when I was working on a project there. We went out, last year, for a couple of months. It ended abruptly."

"After the accident?"

"It seemed as good an excuse as any to say goodbye to her."

"Not a happy relationship, huh?"

He was glaring again. "You ask too many questions."

She widened her smile. She was thinking of Luisa right then, of how Luisa had told her that *somebody* had to stick with Donovan, had to drag him out into the world again.

"Here's another question for you," she said. "Will you please come with me to Luisa's bar tomorrow night?"

He made a humphing sound. "Didn't I already say no—and more than once?"

"What can I tell you? I'm an eternal optimist."

"Lot of good that's doing you."

Still craned around the edge of her computer screen, she braced her elbow on the edge of the desk and rested her chin on the heel of her hand. "Actually, in spite of everything, I do believe I'm making progress with you."

"Oh. Now I'm a job you've taken on, is that it? Something that either goes well, or doesn't?"

"Hmm. It's an interesting way of putting it—but no. You're not a job, Donovan. You're just someone I like. Very much. No matter that you act like an ass a lot of the time."

He grunted. "I'm an ass—but you *like* me."

"That's right. And deep inside you, there's a good man. A good man trying very hard to get out."

"Don't bet any hard cash on that."

"Come with me. Tomorrow night. It will be fun."

"I doubt that."

"Come anyway."

He slanted her a sideways look and muttered, "I'll drive."

"Am I awake? Or is this a dream? I could swear you just said yes."

* * *

Friday night, Abilene wore jeans that clung to every curve. The jeans were tucked into calf-high boots. Her silk blouse was the exact golden-green of her eyes. And her jacket was the same camel color as her boots. Metal-studded leather bangle bracelets, several of them, graced her slim arms.

Donovan thought she looked great. Sexy as hell and ready for anything.

They went together into his underground garage. He wheeled along beside her down the ramp toward the van, still not quite believing that he'd let her talk him into going with her tonight.

"Need any help?" she asked when he stopped several feet back from the rear of the van, took a remote from his pocket and pushed the button that unlocked the doors.

"No. Just get in." He pushed another button and the back doors swung wide. The lift extended out from the van floor and lowered itself to the concrete.

She was still at his side. "Wow. I guess you have it all under control, huh?"

He only wished. He sent her a quelling look. "Get in."

She did, striding away on those amazing legs of hers. He waited until she pulled open the passenger door and swung herself up into the seat. As she shut her door, he rolled onto the platform and let the lift take him up to the floor of the van. From there, he wheeled along the cleared space between the seats and in behind the wheel. He drove from his chair.

They rode in silence most of the way. That was fine with him. Conversation with her could be dangerous. The past few days, he never knew what she was going to talk him into next.

Plus, he kept thinking about sex now, whenever he was around her—okay, maybe he'd *always* thought about sex when he was around her. Subconsciously, anyway.

But since Monday—specifically, since he'd seen her in the shower—he could no longer pretend that sex wasn't on his mind when he looked at her.

And to be brutally frank about it, he didn't even need to be looking at her. She didn't need to be anywhere nearby.

Suddenly, he was thinking about sex all the time. About *having* sex. With her.

Twice in the past few days, in the studio, he'd gotten hard. He was lucky both times, since he was sitting at his desk. All he had to do was to keep on sitting there until the problem subsided.

Still, he found the situation humiliating. All those months and months without a twitch. And now, all of a sudden, he couldn't sit at his own damn desk without a raging woody.

She hadn't known what was happening, he was sure.

And he was grateful for that, at least.

If she'd noticed what was going on with him, she probably would have insisted they discuss it. Frankly. At length. In excruciating detail.

Discussing his current state of continuous arousal with her was the last thing he needed.

"There it is." She pointed at the turnoff up ahead. Beyond it, he could see the red neon sign: Luisa's Cantina, complete with matching zigzagging arrow pointing down at the front doors. The dirt parking lot was packed with pickups and SUVs, and glaringly lit by sodium vapor lamps. "You need to turn."

"Abilene. I know. I've been there before."

She slanted him a frown. "You are edgy tonight, even more so than usual."

He didn't answer her. He concentrated on turning off the highway and then into the lot and then on looking for a decent parking space—easily found, since Luisa had a few handicapped spaces not far from the door.

Men and women in jeans and boots stood out on the wide wooden porch that jutted off the front of the barn-like structure. They lounged against the raw pine railing, wearing jackets against the night chill. Even in the van, with the windows up, he could hear the country-western music from inside, muffled, but clearly distinguishable.

He eased the van in between two extended cabs, each with a handicapped sign dangling from its rearview mirror. The space was a few feet from the wheelchair access ramp. The special parking spaces and the ramp had been there for as long as he'd known Luisa. Even back when he could walk unassisted, he'd always noticed such things. It was part of his job, to include handicapped access in any public building he designed. But this was the first time he would be making use of it himself.

He glanced at Abilene in the seat beside him. In a cheerful clatter of bangle bracelets, she flipped a swatch of chestnut hair back over her shoulder—and winked at him. It annoyed him no end that he found that silly wink of hers sexy.

"Ready?" she asked.

Strangely, he *was* ready.

The edginess she'd remarked on as they left the highway had gone. He might be the only guy in a wheelchair to show up here tonight. Six months ago, he would not have been able to imagine himself doing this. He'd told himself then that he simply never would.

Now, thanks in no small part to the maddening and

relentless woman beside him, he *was* here. And he was going farther. He was wheeling up that ramp and through the front door.

Maybe he would even have a good time. At any rate, it would be something of an adventure. A first.

He gave Abilene a nod.

"Well, all right then." She leaned on her door and swung those long legs to the ground.

He unhooked the locks that held his chair in place and backed cleanly between the seats to the lift. Once he'd ridden it out and down, he used the remote to close everything up again and engage the locks. Abilene was right there, waiting for him.

They headed for the ramp. A few of the cowboys on the front porch were watching them. Maybe they'd never seen a fully equipped wheelchair-ready van before. Maybe they were wondering if the guy in the chair would get up and dance—or maybe just admiring the way Abilene filled out those skinny jeans of hers.

Donovan decided it didn't matter. Whatever they were thinking was their business. There were nods and tipped hats as he and Abilene reached the top of the ramp.

One of the cowboys ambled over and held open the door. Donovan didn't need anyone holding a door for him. He preferred others to ask if he wanted help. Or to wait until he requested it.

But still, he got that the cowboy was only being polite. He gave him an extra nod and a muttered, "Thanks," as he wheeled on through into the din of Luisa's place on a Friday night.

The cantina was just as he remembered: rough plank floors and a long mahogany bar on the far wall, with mirrors behind, a never-ending supply of booze on glass shelves, and ten spigots for various beers on tap. Round tables with bentwood chairs rimmed the dance floor.

Luisa spotted them right away. She'd always been like that. She knew who came into her cantina and she knew when. She hustled on over, wearing jeans as tight as Abilene's and a red off-the-shoulder T-shirt, with Luisa's in black glitter emblazoned across her breasts.

"You came! I'm so happy!" Her smile was wide and her arms were outstretched. She hugged Abilene first. And then she came at him. When she bent down, he allowed her to wrap her arms around him. "Donovan. Oh, it has been much too long since I've seen you here." Her black hair brushed his cheek and she smelled, as always, of jasmine. She stood tall and braced her fists on her hips. "I saved you a table. See? I knew you would come. This way..."

Rounded hips swaying, she led them to a table not far from the bar and swept the reserved sign away. He asked for scotch. Abilene said she would have the same.

Luisa signaled for the drinks and took the chair beside him. She asked them how their work was going and then listened with half an ear as Abilene told her. Luisa was like that, in the bar. Always ready with the hugs and the questions. But as a rule, she hardly heard the answers. Inevitably, she would have to jump up and go deal with another friend who'd just arrived, or handle some mini-crisis or other.

The drinks came. And Luisa left them.

They sipped scotch and listened to the music, watched the locals two-stepping out on the floor. It was nice, easy. Relaxed. If someone had told him two weeks ago that he'd be sitting in Luisa's with Abilene tonight, thoroughly enjoying himself, he would have called them certifiable.

Abilene leaned close to him. "Don't you wish you'd done this sooner?" Her hair swung forward. He could smell her fresh, tart scent—like green apples, watermelon and roses, all somehow perfectly blended together. He wanted to touch her hair. He wanted it bad.

And he had a thousand reasons why he shouldn't have what he wanted.

Screw all those reasons.

He lifted his hand from the table and caught a thick lock between his fingers. Warm. Silky.

He lifted it to his face, took in the scent, the feel, the essence of her. She made no protest—in fact, she leaned marginally closer. He heard her breath catch on a soft hitch of sound.

She didn't ask what was going on, what he was up to—she didn't say a word. That surprised him. She was always so ready to dissect and discuss his every action. But for once, she just let it be. He appreciated that.

It gave him permission, gave him the freedom, to do what he did next.

Which was to touch her cheek, to run the back of his index finger down the perfect curve, to feel the velvet-soft flesh, the elegant shape of her cheekbone beneath.

She sighed.

He wanted to kiss her, to feel the give, the texture, the heat of her mouth. To taste her, to know the warmth of her breath.

She said his name, "Donovan," on a whisper of sound. And he thought that no one, ever, had said his name the way she did. With tenderness. And complete understanding.

With acceptance. And the sweet heat of honest desire.

She leaned in just that fraction closer, a movement that told him she would welcome his kiss.

There was nothing else, at that moment. No one else in the crowded, noisy roadhouse. Just Abilene. So close to him, leaning closer.

He took her mouth. Gently. Lightly.

It wasn't the time or the place for a deep kiss.

But a tender one, yes.

A gentle brush of his mouth to hers was enough—enough to tell him everything he needed to know right then. That her lips were as soft and giving as he'd always known they would be, that the scent of her only got better, sweeter, more tempting, when he was tasting her, too.

With aching reluctance, he pulled back—not far. A few inches. Enough that he could see her eyes again: rich gold, lush green.

He ran a finger down the side of her throat, felt her slight shiver that said she wanted more. She wanted everything. And he thought of the thousand and one ways he had refused her since that first day, that first moment, when she entered the studio. All the small and petty cruelties, which in the end had served no purpose beyond forestalling the inevitable: the two of them, now.

Tonight.

Luisa came back to them, laughing, happy, all busyness and bustle. She dropped into the chair she had vacated a few minutes before. "So sorry to desert you. There's always too much to do here, for me, on a Friday night."

"No problem." Abilene sent Luisa a smile. And then she turned to him again. She met his eyes, glanced down at his mouth. He felt that glance as a physical caress, as if she had kissed him a second time. "We're doing fine."

"Ah." Luisa was catching on. "Yes. I see that you are doing just great. And I'm very pleased." She sounded smug, as if she herself had engineered it all—the evening, the moment, that perfect, brushing kiss.

He probably should have said something cool and ironic. But right then, the last thing he felt was cool. And irony seemed only another defense, another sad little way to reject all the basic human connections he'd set himself on denying.

For tonight, at least, for the short time he and Abilene would have together, he was going to let down his defenses. He was going to let the inevitable find him.

At last.

So he only smiled at Luisa and she grinned back at him and the band started playing a slow, romantic song.

Under the table, Abilene's hand found his, lifted it over the wheel between them and rested it on her knee. They twined their fingers, held on tight. Like a couple of kids in love for the first time, with their whole lives ahead of them, with the world before them, theirs to claim.

"I'll be back," said Luisa, and she jumped up again and headed off toward the bar.

Abilene squeezed his hand. "Want to play some pool?"

He'd taken the armrests off the chair before he left the house. It was easier to work the wheels without them, easier to get around in confined spaces. And also, as luck would have it, to get up close to a pool table to make a shot. "Eight ball?"

"Whatever you say." She leaned in close. He couldn't resist—didn't want to resist. Again, he brushed her lips with his. Her eyes drifted shut—and so did his. She was the one who pulled back that time. She whispered, "I have to warn you, I'm pretty good."

"I'll do my best. I just hope I can hold my own."

Her gaze sharpened. "You're acting much too humble. I can see I might be in trouble here."

"Want to back out?"

"No way. We're playing."

And they did. It was the second time he'd played since the accident on the mountain. The first had been that past Tuesday night, when Alan stayed over.

He'd discovered right away that there were advantages to playing from a wheelchair. Players on two legs had to bend over to get the right angle to line up a shot. From the chair, he was in a good position to begin with.

He and Abilene played best of three. She *was* pretty good. She won the first game.

He took the other two.

After that, there were coins lined up to challenge him. Abilene claimed a stool a few feet from the table and cheered him on. He beat three comers and then a tall blonde in a straw cowboy hat and studded jeans, with colorful tattoos covering both arms stepped up.

She took him down, two in a row.

He shook her hand.

She tipped her hat at him and chalked her cue for the next game.

By then, it was almost midnight. The table they'd had when they arrived was taken, so they found another. Luisa brought them a second round, sat with them for a few minutes, then took off again.

On the dance floor, couples swayed, dancing close and slow. He felt a small stab of regret—that he couldn't rise to his feet, take Abilene's hand, lead her out there and pull her into his arms.

Someday, he might be able to dance again. A slow number anyway, like the one playing now, the kind of dancing where you pretty much just swayed in place. But not in the near future. Not for months, anyway.

Maybe never.

That hadn't bothered him, until tonight. He hadn't given dancing so much as a thought since the accident. It was like sex, something that held no interest for him, something he'd left behind.

Abilene took his hand again, calling him back.

Into the moment, into tonight.

He looked at her. Never would he grow tired of looking at her. "You about ready to go?"

She squeezed his fingers, nodded.

Luisa appeared from the crowd as they worked their way to the door. She bent down and hugged him, pressed a kiss on his cheek. "Come back soon."

He promised that he would.

The drive home was as silent as the ride out there had been. Now, though, it was a silence of anticipation. There was a certain promise between them now, a promise made in a kiss, in the simple act of holding hands.

In the weeks she'd lived in his house, they'd done a lot of talking.

But tonight was like that night almost a week ago, when they'd shared dinner in quiet companionship. Tonight was a night they didn't need words.

When they reached the house, he followed the driveway around to the garage entrance. They were in and parked, the engine idling, when she leaned across the space between her seat and his chair.

"My rooms?" she asked him, her face tipped up to his, her skin pearly in the dim glow from the dashboard lights. Her mouth, her husky voice, her night-dark eyes, the scent of her—*all* of her—invited him.

She made a low sound as their lips met. And she opened for him.

He swept his tongue in, groaning at the taste of her, the wet, tempting slickness. She put her hand on his shoulder, clasping, holding on to him.

That did it.

He was aching for her, growing hard.

She pulled back. Her eyes seemed haunted, a trick of the dim light. "My rooms?" she asked again.

His throat clutched. He felt absurdly inexperienced, as though this were his first time—which, in a sense, it was. Somehow, he managed a nod.

She reached out again, bangle bracelets clattering, her hand sliding warm and smooth against his nape, to pull him close for one last, hard, swift kiss.

And then, as quick as she had kissed him, she released him. She leaned on her door and swung those long legs out. She jumped down, pushed the door shut between them.

For a moment, she stood out there, beside the van, looking in at him, as if she had something important to say. But in the end, she only turned and left him.

He pivoted in his chair, tracking her, watching her walk away around the end of the van, her boot heels tapping out a hollow rhythm on the concrete floor.

She headed for the ramp. Too soon, she was out of sight.

Once he could no longer see her, he had the strangest sensation—that he had lost her already, without ever letting himself have her. That tonight hadn't really happened. That he was alone.

Again.

That, he couldn't bear. Not now. Not yet.

He was backed out and down in record time. He shut up the van and made for the exit ramp as fast as his wheels would carry him.

Chapter Nine

In her rooms, Abilene worked fast.

She took off her bangles and dropped them on the table by the bed. She took off her jacket, her shirt, her bra. Perched on the stool at the end of the bed, she tore off her boots, her jeans—everything. Naked, she grabbed the clothes in her arms, carried them to the closet, tossed them inside and shut the door.

And then yanked it open again.

Maybe greeting him naked was a little too...much.

She dug around in the pile of clothes until she found her silk panties. Once she'd wiggled back into them, she went to the dresser in the middle of the closet, where she started opening drawers and riffling through them, looking for something that was attractive, but maybe not too overtly seductive.

Not that she'd brought anything overtly seductive.

After all, she'd come here to work, not to have sex with Donovan.

In the end, she settled on the one nightgown she'd brought. It was cotton, a warm bronze color, very thin and wispy. It left her arms bare, but covered the rest of her to her ankles.

Not sexy, really. But not exactly unsexy. And certainly not as bad as greeting him in her Rice T-shirt and tattered sweats.

The bed was already turned back. Olga did that, nightly. So she ran around the sitting room, the bedroom and the bathroom, getting the lighting right—low, but not *too* low.

By then, a good ten minutes had passed since she left him in the garage. He would be knocking on the sitting room door any second now.

Wouldn't he?

He'd better be.

She went out to the sitting room and perched on the couch, where she stared at the door to the hallway, willing that knock to come.

It didn't. Endless seconds ticked by.

Eventually, she jumped up and went back to the bedroom, to check the time on the bedside clock: fifteen full minutes had gone by since he agreed to meet her in her room.

She went back to the sitting room, stood in the middle of the floor and tried to figure out what to do next.

What was going on here? He *had* agreed he would come to her rooms. Hadn't he?

He'd agreed with a nod, which clearly meant yes. But maybe she should have insisted that he say it out loud.

Then again, if he'd changed his mind after the fact, what difference did it make?

She paced the floor, trying to decide what her next move should be. Should she go to his rooms? Call him?

Or just forget it? Just take off this not-quite-sexy nightgown, put on her sweats and go to bed.

The knock—three light taps—cut her off in midpace.

In a rush, she released the breath she hadn't even realized she was holding. She considered calling out that the door was open. But then she ended up racing over there and turning the knob.

At the last second, she decided she'd better be sure it was him before she swung the door wide. When it came to Donovan, well, a woman just never knew….

So she peeked around the edge of the door.

And there he was, staring back at her, still wearing the same sweater and jeans he'd worn to Luisa's. One side of that wonderful mouth of his kicked up. "Changed your mind?"

"I most certainly did not." She stepped back, pulling the door wide. "I was getting a little worried about *you,* though."

He wheeled in.

Once he'd cleared the threshold, she shut the door and leaned back against it, turning the lock by feel, her knees suddenly rubbery and her chest kind of tight. "Is everything all right?"

"Abilene."

"What?" She sounded snippy. Somehow, she couldn't help herself.

"I went to my room, that's all. To get condoms."

She realized she'd failed to mention that they didn't need them. "I'm on the pill." Then again, well, you couldn't be too safe these days. "But I guess it's wise, to use a condom in any case."

"Well, all right, then." He looked her up and down, a lazy kind of look, a look that took its sweet time. When his eyes rose to meet hers again, he started backing the chair toward the center of the room. "Come away from the door." He said it softly, with wonderful, delicious intent.

And she felt instantly better about everything. It was obvious that he wanted to be with her. She could stop feeling that maybe she had pushed him into something he just wasn't ready for.

She took a cautious step.

"Nice nightgown," he said. He sounded like he really meant it.

But she felt suddenly shy anyway. She gnawed on her lower lip, fiddled with the wide straps that held up the top. "It's not exactly seductive…."

"It's perfect."

She felt a flush flooding up her neck and over her cheeks, and she had to look away. "I, um, thank you."

"Come here."

She took another step. "I feel…kind of awkward, you know? As if it's my first time, or something, which it's not. I mean, it's not like there were a *lot* of guys, or anything. But still, it's not as if I'm a virgin or anything…." She shut her mouth, swallowed. Yikes. Talk about an excess of information.

"I know what you mean." He said it low, roughly tender. "When you kissed me in the van, I was thinking that I felt completely out of my depth, like it was my first time all over again."

"You did?"

"Yeah. And it *is* the first time. *Our* first time."

Now she almost wanted to cry. "Oh, Donovan…"

"Yeah?"

"That was the perfect thing to say."

"You think so?" He looked kind of pleased with himself.

"I do, yes. The perfect thing."

"So you think you might come all the way over here, then?"

She did just that, stopping inches from his front wheels. He put his palms to his thighs, patted gently. She hesitated. "Will I…hurt you?"

"I'll let you know if it gets too bad."

"So it *will* hurt you, hurt your legs, if I sit on your lap?"

"If it does, a little, it will be worth it." He engaged the brake, locking the wheels into place. "Trust me to tell you, if something isn't going to work for me."

"Yes, all right." Her throat felt constricted. And her heart was just jackhammering away inside her chest. She could almost laugh at herself. She'd been so confident, at Luisa's, and when she kissed him down in the garage. Where had all that boldness gone?

But then he held out his hand to her.

She took it. And she found reassurance, in the steadiness and strength of his grip. She let herself relax a little, let herself feel again the electric excitement that charged the air between them every time they touched.

He gave a tug. She took his signal, gathering her nightgown in her free hand, lifting it high enough to get it out of her way. It was so simple, to hitch one leg over him, to slide her hips forward, so she straddled his lap.

With slow care, she settled her weight onto him, the skirt of her gown riding high across the tops of her thighs.

"You feel good," he said. He let go of her hand and clasped her bare thigh. Heat shimmered through her as he stroked her skin with his open palm. "Smooth."

She framed his face in her hands. "Oh, Donovan…"

"Shh," he said. "It's all right." And he kissed her, a slow, deep kiss, wet and sweet and so arousing.

His tongue slid over hers, retreating, and then gliding forward again, beneath hers that time, in a slick caress that brought a soft moan into her throat. The kiss went on and on and he touched her as he kissed her, first with long, exploratory caresses of her bare thighs. And then, more deliberately.

He cupped her bent knees in his palms. And after that, he took the caress lower, down the sensitive, thin flesh of her shins, and around, to learn the curves of her calves, the secret coves behind her knees.

She touched him, too. She ran her eager hands along the hard, thick muscles of his shoulders, over his chest, so deep and powerful, heavy with muscle even through the soft wool of the sweater he wore. Encircling his neck, she let her touch stray up into his close-cut hair. The short strands were warm, alive, between her fingers.

And then he ended the kiss, pulling away just enough that their lips no longer met. He pressed his forehead to hers. With a long, slow sigh, she braced her forearms on his shoulders and linked her hands behind his head.

Below, she could feel him. Growing hard. She tried moving her hips on him in a gentle, rocking motion.

It felt so good, she sighed again, let her head fall back and groaned his name, "Donovan…"

He pressed his lips to her throat, grazed the sensitive skin there with his teeth. "Yes…"

And then those wonderful strong hands of his were sliding under the hem of her nightgown, around the sides of her thighs. He cupped her bottom, over her panties, and he urged her to move faster—and then slower. And then faster again.

And again, they were kissing, mouths fused and hungry, as she moved on him, creating the sweetest, hottest kind of friction, and she was burning, deliciously. She was on fire, a fire that only flared hotter, that built and spread, all through her.

He tasted so good. He *felt* so good.

She let her hands stray downward, along his sides, so lean and compact, to his tight waist. For a moment, she lingered there, her hips rocking, her hands on either side of him, holding on good and tight, as the pleasure within her built in fiery waves.

Beneath his sweater, she felt his warmth. But she wanted more. So she took the sweater by the hem and tugged it upward. For a moment, he resisted, unwilling to let go of her.

But she was insistent. And finally, he gave in. He eased his hands from the folds of her nightgown and lifted his arms high.

With a moan, she pulled her mouth from his and whipped the sweater up between them. He did the rest, yanking it all the way off, tossing it to the floor.

And then they were kissing again. And he had those hands of his back under her gown, holding her, urging her onward.

And she was rocking him, rocking herself, rocking both of them, as she wrapped her arms around him, ran her hungry fingers up and down the hard muscles of his back.

She could have gone on like that forever, moving against him as he kissed her in that so thorough, so lazy, slow, delicious way he had. He still had his jeans on. She still wore her panties. But even with the barrier of their clothing between them, it felt perfect to her.

It felt absolutely right.

But he took it further. He trailed a hand slowly, up under her nightgown, along the lower curve of her back... and around.

To the front of her again. He pressed his palm flat against her belly. And then those skilled fingers of his slid lower.

He cupped her.

She froze. And she gasped.

He took that soft sound into him as he eased his fingers under the elastic of her panties and slid them into the wetness between her thighs.

Oh, it felt so good. So thrilling, so free. So exactly right.

She was open to him and he stroked her, continuing to cup her at the same time, holding her in place with one hand as with the other he did the most amazing, lovely things. He dipped a finger in, then two. And with his thumb, he found her sweet spot.

Oh, she was losing it. She hovered in a haze of building pleasure, on the far edge. She teetered on the verge of completion.

And then, she was there. She was going over. The soft explosion claimed her.

She grabbed his wrist, widened her legs even farther, held on tight, moaned low and helplessly, deep in her throat as the sweet, shimmering contractions took her. The pleasure increased in waves, taking her higher, and yet higher still. Until she hit the second peak, surged over it...and down.

The slow fade-off began.

She sagged against him, murmuring wordless things, boneless now.

He gathered her close to him, wrapping his arms around her. She felt the brushing touch of his lips in her hair, the warmth of his breath at her temple. For a time they just sat there, in his chair, together. Entwined.

Some time passed. Minutes. Forever.

When she finally lifted her head from his shoulder, he touched her cheek and she met his shining eyes. He stroked her hair, guided a heavy, tangled lock of it behind her ear.

They shared another kiss—a tender one, a light brushing of his mouth to hers.

And then he was gathering her nightgown in his hands, easing it up. She raised her arms and he pulled it off and away, dropping it to the floor on top of his sweater.

"So fine," he whispered, bending his head to touch his tongue to the tip of one breast. He pressed his thumbs to either side of her navel, holding her waist in his hands. And then he caressed his way upward, until he cradled both breasts.

She sighed and arched her back, offering him total access. He took it, bending closer, taking one nipple into his mouth, swirling his hot tongue around it, and then sinking his teeth in—not too hard, just enough to add to her pleasure.

He kissed her other breast, too, taking his time about it, making her moan again, making her clutch his big shoulders and whisper his name.

And then his hands were around her waist again, lifting.

She took his cue and transferred her weight to her toes. A little unsteadily, with her legs spread so wide, she started to rise. He helped her, taking most of her weight in his two strong hands. She hitched one leg back and then the other, clearing the large rear wheels of the chair. And then the smaller front wheels, too. At last she was able to find her balance upright, to bring her legs together.

He gazed up at her, his eyes heavy-lidded. She smiled down at him, admiring the beautiful musculature of his arms and shoulders, the hard perfection of his chest and belly. Such a gorgeous man.

And still very much aroused, his hardness straining the fly of his jeans.

He canted forward then, touched the side of her hip, tracing the curve of it, following the shape of her, up into the cove of her waist, and then back down again. Little flares of heat burst along her skin in the most wonderful way, wherever he touched her.

He took hold of the bits of elastic at her hips and eased her panties down, over her thighs, to her knees. Then he sat back again. She did the rest, bending to slide them down all the way, stepping out of them, using her toe to kick them aside.

She rose to her height again.

Naked, she thought. *I'm standing here naked in front of Donovan McRae.*

And then she grinned to herself, as she realized that his seeing her naked really wasn't anything new.

"I know what you're thinking," he said, low and rough.

"Maybe you do."

Or maybe he didn't.

It made no difference.

What mattered was that they were here, together, in this intimate way. What mattered was that it was good, between them. It was honest. Open. True.

He said, "You're so beautiful. I never thought this would happen."

"I didn't, either. But it did. It is. And Donovan, I'm so glad that you're here with me...."

He asked, "The bed?"

She shook her head. "I was thinking, the first time, we could try it in your chair...."

His eyes grew darker. Softer. "Sure." His hands were already at his fly. He unbuttoned, unzipped.

"Can I help?"

He lifted one sculpted shoulder in a half-shrug. "I guess it would make things quicker."

"Your shoes?"

"Thanks. Yeah."

So she bent on one knee and took off his shoes for him, and also his socks. When she stood again, he'd taken the condoms from a pocket. He held them out to her. She set two on the nightstand, and kept the other, ready, in her hand.

With some effort, he began easing down his jeans and underwear. She stepped back a little. Partly to admire the view. Partly because if he wanted help, he would say so.

He paused with the jeans and briefs still high on his thighs and he snared her glance, held it, his square jaw suddenly tight. "You should be warned. It's not a very pretty sight...."

She only looked at him, steadily, without wavering. It seemed to her that there were no words for this. Her complete acceptance of him was what mattered, her ability to communicate that she wanted him exactly as he was, that the man he was now, at this minute, was enough for her—more than enough.

He braced his feet on the footrest and with a groan

he tried to stifle, lifted his hips enough to take the jeans down to his thighs. Since he didn't ask for more help from her, she didn't offer it.

Bending at the waist, he pushed the jeans and briefs over his knees, down his calves and, finally, all the way off. And then he wadded them tight and tossed them away from him.

Slowly, he sat up straight again. He remained hard, fully aroused. She had absolutely no doubt that he wanted her.

But his eyes had turned wary. He was watching her, gauging her reaction to the sight of his damaged legs. "Pretty ugly, huh?"

"No," she said. "Not ugly at all."

"Liar." But at least he said it with a tender smile.

She wanted to argue, to promise she wasn't lying, that his legs weren't ugly. But why go there? They were what they were. And in comparison to the buff perfection of his upper body, they did look sad and wasted—the right leg especially. It was much worse than the left, criss-crossed with ridges of scar tissue, some of it red and angry, the long rows of stitches still visible. His calves were too thin, his ankles slightly swollen.

He gave a low chuckle. "A lot of pins, rods and screws involved, putting them in, taking them out again. Believe it or not, this whole mess looks a hell of a lot better than it did just a month ago…."

"I believe it."

He searched her face, seeking the slightest hint that she might be having second thoughts—about tonight, about the two of them.

But she had none. And he must have seen that.

Because he held out his hand to her again.

She took it, and she came to him, easing a leg over

him, straddling him as she had before—only now, there was nothing, not the slightest scrap of fabric, between them. They were flesh to flesh.

She kissed him, sliding her fingers free of his, peeling the wrapper off the condom and then slipping her hand between them and down, so she could encircle him. He moaned into her mouth when her grip closed around him.

He was silky. So hard. So warm. She moved her hips in rhythm with her stroking hand.

As she stroked him, he clasped her thighs, his fingers gliding underneath, so he could caress her from below. She felt her own wetness, her readiness for him.

And then he was lifting her, taking some of her weight on his arms. She helped him, rising to her toes, moving in closer against him, so her breasts brushed his chest and her toes, behind the rear wheels, could touch the floor.

She still had her hand down between them, around him, and she moved it lower, to the base of him, so she could hold him in place. She rolled the condom over him.

There. It was on.

She tipped her hips forward, lifting them. He helped her, raising her higher, into position to take him inside.

Yes. Just…there.

She felt him, so sleek and hot, nudging her, parting her.

With a long, hungry moan, she lowered herself onto him. He came into her in a sweet, hot glide. Her body put up no resistance. She welcomed him.

There was only pleasure. Only heat.

Only the delicious, complete, thrilling way he filled her.

She let her head fall back and a deep cry escaped her;

it felt so very good. And he leaned into her, kissed her throat, her chin, opening his mouth on her, licking her, scraping her burning skin lightly with his teeth…

Until she lowered her head and offered her lips. He took them. She parted to him eagerly, gave herself over to his deep, wet kiss.

With his powerful arms supporting her thighs, giving her something to brace against, she could take control. And she did. She moved on him in deep, hard strokes and he helped her, lifting when her body signaled him, lowering when she pushed down.

He felt so good, so exactly right.

And behind her eyes there was darkness, beautiful darkness. Darkness turning slowly to blinding, glorious light.

Chapter Ten

Donovan woke in Abilene's bed.

For a moment, he lay there, eyes closed, unmoving.

Remembering.

Every kiss. Every whispered endearment. Every hot, sweet caress.

It had been good. Damn good. Better, even, than in all his frustrated fantasies of how it might be.

He opened his eyes. He lay on his side, facing her. His legs hurt. But then, they always did.

She was still sleeping—on her back, one slim pale arm thrown across her eyes, her hair wild on the pillow, her lips slightly parted. Her breathing was shallow. Quiet. Slow.

He ached to touch her, to take hold of the blankets, pull them away slowly. To reveal every inch of her, every hollow, every soft, inviting curve.

It made him hard all over again, just thinking about

something so simple as easing the blankets down so he could see her bare breasts. But the clock on the nightstand said it was nine-fifteen. Long past time that they should be up and at work.

Yes, it was Saturday. And yes, she deserved a day off.

But they couldn't afford that. They had two weeks and two days left until the agreed-upon presentation to the Foundation people. They were making fine progress.

But still, the timeline was an impossibly short one. There would be no days off.

She rolled her head his way, lowered her arm and opened one eye. "Oh, God. I know that look. It's the *get to work* look."

"We should have been up hours ago."

She groaned. "Can't I have just one kiss, please? Before you start cracking the whip again."

He eased a strand of hair out of the corner of her soft mouth. "It's after nine."

"Ugh."

"Work."

"Have I told you lately that I hate you?"

He grinned. "You don't have to tell me. I can see it in your eyes." And then he sat up, pushed the covers off his scarred legs and eased them, with great care, over the edge of the bed.

"You're such a romantic the morning after," she grumbled behind him.

He sent her a glance over his shoulder. "Don't tempt me."

"I wouldn't dream of it." She looked right in his eyes and she eased down the blankets. Her full breasts with their pretty, puckered nipples came into view.

He was the one groaning then. "Unfair."

She laughed, a low, husky sound that stirred him even more than her nudity. And then she sighed and pulled the covers up again. "You're right. We need to work."

He continued to stare at her. He really liked staring at her. It felt good—freeing—to be able to do it openly now.

Finally, he shook himself and reached for his chair, which waited where he'd left it, next to the bed. It was easy, after all the months of practice, to lift himself into the seat using only his arms.

She was shaking her head as he dropped neatly into place. "It's amazing, watching you do that."

"It's all about upper-body strength and conditioning. Nothing any gymnast can't do and do well."

"Still, it doesn't seem humanly possible."

"I'm a fortunate man. I have my own personal gym and I can afford to hire good trainers. All I had to do was put in the time."

Her expression had turned chiding. "Don't minimize what you've accomplished, Donovan."

"All right, I won't. I'm amazing."

Her eyes went soft. "Yeah. You are. You definitely are."

He wanted to swing himself back into that bed with her. But no. Not an option. There was work that needed doing, work that wouldn't wait. "So, mind if I use your bathroom—just for a few minutes?"

"Be my guest. Take your time."

He backed and turned and aimed himself at the bathroom.

When he came out again, she was wearing sweats and a Rice T-shirt. His briefs, jeans and sweater were laid out neatly across the bench at the foot of the bed, his shoes and socks lined up beside them. He wheeled over there. "Thanks."

She nodded. "Need any help?"

"No, I can manage."

"I'm going to take a shower, then." She headed for the bathroom, pausing in the doorway. "Breakfast in the studio?"

"Yeah. We can eat while we work."

The day was a good one, Abilene thought. A very productive one.

Their routine was the same as it had been. She worked steadily, and he worked with her for a couple of hours that morning. Then, as always, he left her to continue on her own and he went to spend time in the gym. He returned briefly before lunch to check on her progress and make suggestions. Then he was gone again. Lunch, like breakfast, she had in the studio while she worked.

Donovan appeared again around three.

Anyone observing them that day might have thought everything was the same between them. As before, he demanded much of her. He could be very tough, and if he didn't like something she'd come up with, he told her what he wanted changed in no uncertain terms.

And she talked right back to him, same as she always had. He might be a genius and she might be really grateful to have this chance to work with him. But no way was she letting him get all up in her face. She demanded respect, too. And she could give as good as she got.

So everything between them was the same.

Except that it wasn't.

Now they were lovers.

Just the thought of that, of the simple words, *He is my lover,* brought a thrilling, heated shiver running beneath her skin. And every time she looked at him, she felt that little lurch in her belly, that click of recognition, that deeper knowledge a woman has of the man who shares her bed.

She worked hard and she kept her focus.

But still, through the whole day, she felt a rising sensation, a sweet anticipation. She wanted him.

And she would have him when the workday was through.

At five, when she was ready to stop for the day, he was in the studio with her, over behind that volcanic slab of a desk of his, puzzling through an issue with storage room access.

She straightened her work area and got up to leave. "I'm going for a swim. I'll see you at dinner."

He glanced up. Their gazes met. The shimmery, heated feeling within her grew brighter, hotter.

She wanted to run to him, to bend close to him, fuse her mouth to his. The answering flare of heat in his eyes told her he was thinking along similar lines.

But no. It was better, wiser, to wait.

The studio was their workplace. And she'd been tempted all day to give in to her desire for him and blatantly try to seduce him in that very room. Maybe on that enormous desk of his.

It should be possible. If he could manage to swing himself up there, she could do the rest....

Uh-uh. No. Better if she disciplined herself in here, during work, from the first.

"Dinner," she said again.

He gave a low, knowing laugh that sent little flares of bright heat exploding along her nerve endings. "Dinner. Got it."

She turned and headed for the door before she ended up behaving in a manner that was totally undisciplined.

"Your brother-in-law called me," Donovan said during dinner.

By then, they'd had their salad and Olga had just served the lamb chops and the lemon tarragon asparagus. Everything was delicious, as always, but all Abilene could think about was getting the man across from her alone.

For a moment she wondered which brother-in-law. Pretty pitiful, considering she only had one—a brand-new one, Dax Girard—who had married her baby sister Zoe at New Year's. "Uh. Dax, you mean?"

Donovan nodded. "He gave me a hard time for not taking his calls."

"I'm glad," she said gently, "that you finally did talk with him. Did you tell him what you've been through in the past year?"

"That I'm using a wheelchair now—is that what you mean?" He phrased the sentence as a question. But it wasn't, not really. It was a put-down, a warning that he didn't want to be quizzed on what he might have said to Dax about his physical condition.

She ignored the warning. She never would have gotten this far with him if she'd heeded his warnings. "Yes, Donovan. That you use a wheelchair is part of it, of course."

He made a low snorting sound. "Yes, I told him that my legs were badly damaged in the accident on the mountain—worse than I let it be known at first. Badly enough that I'm using a wheelchair now."

She smiled at him, a wide, approving smile. "Good."

He glanced away—to show her he was still annoyed with her? Or maybe to keep from returning her smile? Who knew?

And that he was defensive about what he'd said to Dax really didn't bother her, anyway. She was simply grateful, that he was willing, at last, to talk to his friends, to tell them what was going on with him.

Also, his frankness with her new brother-in-law freed her up to be more honest with her family. She'd yet to explain to them the challenges Donovan faced. It hadn't seemed right, as long as he was so guarded about it. But now, at last, he was letting people know his situation.

She prompted in an offhand tone, "So, what else did you and Dax talk about?"

Now, he turned to look at her again. It was a cool look—or at least, it tried to be. But Abilene knew him better than she once had. His dismissive remarks and icy glances were only defenses, ways to keep the world at bay after whatever had damaged his spirit so badly. Slowly, he was giving those defenses up.

And that was what mattered.

He said, "Dax tried to talk me into visiting him and your sister in San Antonio."

Dax was über-rich. His house, in one of SA's most exclusive areas, was more like a palace. And then there was the giant garage, where he kept his collection of classic and one-of-a-kind vehicles, there was the gorgeous pool, the tennis court….

Abilene sipped her wine and then suggested casually, "We should go."

He dismissed that idea with a lazy shrug. "Not going to happen. You know that."

"Things change. So do people. *You've* changed,

Donovan, just in the few weeks I've known you. You've changed a lot, and for the better."

"I'm not going to San Antonio."

She brushed his objections away. "It's time, and you know it. And not only for you, personally. We're getting to the point where we need to be on-site. We need to bring in the other architects, start working with the builder."

His forbidding expression had only grown more so as she spoke. "What's this 'we'? You know I'm not going to San Antonio with you. You knew it from the start."

She set down her wineglass. "That's another thing I've been meaning to discuss with you."

He was openly sneering now. "You look way too damn determined. I hate it when you get that look."

"I only want you to consider that things are changing—*you* are changing. And for the better."

"You're repeating yourself."

"Some things bear repeating."

"I have not changed."

"You sound like a sulky kid, you know that?"

"Did I mention I don't like where this is going?"

"Too bad. You told me when I got here that you would never work again. Well, Donovan. You *are* working. You're doing amazing work. It's not going to kill you to admit that you are."

He made another snorting sound. "You're doing the work. I'm merely guiding you, giving you a nudge now and then, and only when you need one—which is rarely."

"Oh, please. You're the one who made it all come together. We both know it. You found the heart of this project. And you've been with me, creating it, every step of the way. As a result of what you created, we're actually ahead of our own impossibly tight schedule."

"You're overstating my contribution."

"No, I'm not."

He went on as though she hadn't spoken. "We're almost to the point now where you won't need me. And I took your inexperience into consideration when I chose the firm you'll be working with. The Johnson Wallace Group is the best."

She'd heard of the Johnson Wallace Group, of course. They were based in Dallas and their reputation was worldwide. "Donovan, you're not listening to me."

"I heard every word you said."

"But you weren't *listening*."

He sipped from his water glass. "Of course I was listening. Now, about Johnson Wallace. The two partners in the San Antonio office, Doug Lito and Ruth Gilman, are excellent architects—and they work well with others. You'll be able to count on their support and considerable experience."

"I know Johnson Wallace is the best around. And I've actually met Ruth Gilman and liked her. But that's not the issue."

"There is no issue." He cut off a tender bite of lamb. "It's a brilliant design and you're going to be ready to take over."

She dropped her fork. Hard. It clattered against her china plate. "Donovan. You're not hearing me. My taking over was never the plan, and you know it."

"It's been the plan, and *you* know it. I made that more than clear the first day you got here." He ate the bite of lamb, started cutting another.

She reached out, stilled his hand. "You know what plan I mean. The *original* plan. The plan you proposed to the Help the Children Foundation, the one you offered as a fellowship to me and a bunch of other hopeful beginners. You started this fully intending to be in on it all the way. That was the contract you made with everyone involved and that's why it matters, that you see it through, that you come, too, when it's time to go to San Antonio."

He shrugged off her touch. Then he set down his fork and knife and sat back in his wheelchair. She, on the other hand, sat forward, urgently, *willing* him to see what he needed to do—and to finally agree to do it.

"What are you telling me, really?" His tone was as cutting and cruel as it had ever been. "You're afraid you can't handle it? You're just not up for supervising the construction phase?"

"Oh, I can handle it. Not nearly as well as *we* can, as a team. But well enough to get the job done, especially if Ruth Gilman has my back."

"Then there's no problem."

"Yes. There *is* a problem, the one you keep refusing to talk about. Whether or not I can handle it isn't the question. It was never the question. The question is what's holding you back, what's keeping you from carrying through on the commitment you made?"

He refused to answer her. Instead, he insisted, "There is no point in going on about this. I explained the situation to you the day you got here. You stayed, and by staying you accepted those terms."

"But I only—"

"We're done here."

"But—"

"I said, we're done." He took his napkin from his lap and dropped it on the table next to his half-finished meal. And then he backed and turned and wheeled away from her. She watched as he disappeared through the arch into the front room.

With a discouraged little sigh, Abilene sagged in her chair. She gazed glumly down at her barely touched meal.

So much for how far she and Donovan had come together.

Donovan wheeled fast down the hallway until he reached his own rooms. Once he rolled over the threshold, he spun the chair around, grabbed the door and gave it a shove.

The door was solid core, very heavy. When it slammed, it slammed hard. The sound it made was supremely satisfying to him.

But the satisfaction didn't last.

He pulled a second wheelie, spun the chair again and ended up facing the sitting room fireplace. As well as the portrait hanging above it.

Elias. At two. Before Donovan even really knew him. Wearing some ridiculous little sailor-boy suit Julie had put him in, sitting on a kid-size chair, one plump leg tucked beneath him, clutching his favorite Elmo doll, his chubby face tipped back, laughing at something the photographer—or maybe Julie—must have said or done.

Sometimes, when Donovan looked at that picture, he could still hear the sound of his son's happy laughter. But not often, not anymore. As the years went by, the sound, when he did hear it, seemed to get fainter. A bright, perfect memory fading by slow, painful degrees.

He turned from the portrait, and his defensive fury at Abilene drained away, leaving him feeling foolish and petty and weighed down by regrets. Wheeling on into the bedroom, he avoided letting his gaze fall on the framed snapshot by the bed, of Elias at the beach. Instead, he went on into the bathroom. He turned on the water in the deep, jetted tub and stripped.

The water welcomed him. He sank into it with a long sigh. He closed his eyes and tried not to think about what a jerk he was being, about the evening he might have been having, in Abilene's bed.

Abilene called her mom that night.

She told Aleta Bravo more about Donovan than she'd ever felt comfortable revealing before, including that he used a wheelchair—and that she cared for him. A lot. More so, each day.

Her mom was great, as always, accepting and supportive. She said she hoped she'd be meeting Donovan soon.

After talking to her mom, Abilene called Zoe, who instantly confessed she'd made Dax tell her everything that Donovan had said to him earlier that day.

"Dax tried to get him to come and visit us," Zoe said. "Donovan never quite got around to giving him an answer on the invitation—and he didn't invite us out there to West Texas to see him, either."

"I know. Donovan told me, tonight, during dinner, that Dax had invited him for a visit. And then we had a big fight about it."

"A fight?"

"Long story. Too long—and way too complicated."

"Ab, why do I get the feeling that there's more going on with you two than this fellowship you waited so long for?"

Abilene busted herself. "There *is* more. A lot more."

Zoe said nothing for a moment. And then, when she did speak, she sounded nothing short of philosophical. "Well, I guess I knew this would happen."

"Excuse me?"

"Oh, come on. You've been talking about Donovan McRae for years. You idolize him."

"I idolize Mies van der Rohe, too." Van der Rohe was one of the great pioneers of Modern architecture. "But that doesn't mean I want to get intimate with him."

"Isn't Mies van der Rohe dead?"

"Oh, very funny. You know what I mean."

"So...how serious is it?"

"It feels serious to me. But it's all new, you know?"

"What about kids? Does he want them? *Can* he...?"

"Wait a minute. Didn't I just say it's all new? Do we need to jump right to whether or not he can father a child?"

"You just said it feels serious. And it *is* an issue you would have to deal with—I mean, if you want children."

Abilene sighed. Really, the question didn't strike her as all that rude and tactless, given that it was coming from Zoe. After all, Dax had once sworn that kids and married life were not for him. Zoe had taken him at his word.

And that had created no end of problems between them, as Zoe had come to discover she did want children. Very much.

They'd worked it out and ended up together. And they were expecting their first, a boy, in May. So the big question of having babies—or not having them—was front and center in Zoe's mind.

"Ab, you still with me?"

"I'm here."

"Well?"

Abilene gave in and told her what she wanted to know. "The accident only affected his legs. So yes, as far as I know, he *can.* And yes, I do want kids. And next you'll be asking me if I really think I can deal long-term with a guy who uses a wheelchair."

Zoe made a humphing sound. "No way. I know you. You can deal with anything you set that big brain of yours on accomplishing. If you were a wimp or a quitter or prone to being overwhelmed, yeah, I might ask. But you? Uh-uh—and will you get him to come to SA, please? I want to meet him."

"I'm working on that. So far, as I think I mentioned, it's not going all that well."

Zoe laughed. "You'll make him see the light. I have total faith in you."

"Tell that to Donovan."

"I will, you can count on it—I mean, after I get to know him a little, once you get him to come to SA."

"He says he won't."

"You'll talk him into it. And keep me posted?"

"Will do," Abilene promised. She asked how Zoe was feeling.

"I feel great. You should see me. I actually look pregnant now. It's about time, I guess, almost six months along. And he's started kicking. I think he plans to be a football star." She sounded so happy.

But why wouldn't she be? She had a husband she adored, a baby on the way. And she also worked with Dax, at his magazine, *Great Escapes.* She loved her job. Zoe, the one who could never settle down and stick with anything, had finally found the life that suited her perfectly.

The conversation wound down after that. Zoe said goodbye.

As Abilene got ready for bed, she found herself thinking of Donovan's son again—the son he had never so much as mentioned to her. She'd spent nearly a month working closely with him. She'd made tender, hot love with him last night—and still he hadn't said one word about the lost Elias.

Plus, there was the argument earlier, at the dinner table. She hated that she couldn't get through to him, make him see what he really did need to do. But more than that, she hated that his ultimate solution to a heated disagreement had been to simply wheel away.

She'd told Zoe that this thing with Donovan felt serious to her. And it did. But maybe to Donovan, it just didn't.

It hurt, to consider that he really might not care all that much about what was going on between them. It hurt her heart—and her foolish pride.

In the bedroom, after she'd put on her comfy sweats and brushed her teeth, she considered getting under the covers. But no way would she sleep.

She got some paper and a pencil and did some sketching—just kind of doodling, fooling around with ideas for houses and various other structures she might someday actually get a chance to build. When that got old, she put on some sneakers and went to the kitchen, where she dished up a slice of Anton's blackberry cheesecake. She carried the dessert into the dark studio, turned on all the lights, sat down at her desk and powered up the computer.

For a while, between bites of the creamy treat, she worked on the text of her proposal for the Foundation people. It was descriptive writing, designed to promote the project, to impress the client—in this case, to convince the Foundation that she knew what she was doing, with or without a master architect to guide her.

It didn't go well. Her mind kept wandering, as it had

back in her rooms, to thoughts of Donovan. It seemed she couldn't escape him.

So she switched to the drafting board and her pet project, the one she always turned to when she was troubled or in need of distraction. She had hundreds of drawings of this particular structure already, of varying exterior views, of every room seen from every angle. It was her Hill Country dream house, the one she fantasized about building someday, for the husband and children she didn't have yet.

Sometimes she drew it as a rambling craftsman-style structure; sometimes it had a log cabin exterior. The floorplan kept changing, too, over time. Currently, her dream house was forty-seven hundred square feet—two thousand nine hundred downstairs, and eighteen hundred up. It had a vaulted great room with a floor-to-ceiling natural stone fireplace at one end and a formal dining room at the other. The built-in media center and carved double doors separated the great room from the home office, which had the same wide-plank floors and extensive built-ins. The kitchen, with walk-in pantry, center island and snack-bar counter, opened to a sky-lit second kitchen—an outdoor kitchen—with its own cooktop and oven and corner fireplace.

She was rethinking the purpose of a small interior section between the four-car garage and the outdoor kitchen, when Donovan said, "You're working late."

Her hopeless heart lifted. She glanced up to see him sitting in the doorway at the far end of the room—the door nearest his own desk. "Not working, just...daydreaming, really. Daydreaming on paper."

He rolled the chair, first back a few inches, and then forward, stopping in the center of the doorway, pretty much right where he had started. As if he hesitated to enter his own studio. "I went to your rooms first." It was a confession. "And then I tried the kitchen. When you weren't in either place, I figured maybe here..."

"Ah," she said, a warm glow flowing all through her at the thought that he had come to find her, that he *did* care about her, at least a little. And yet still, she wasn't going to prompt him. If he had something to say to her, he was going to have to get the words out all by himself.

Finally, he did. "I'm sorry, Abilene. I didn't want to hear what you had to say at dinner. And when you wouldn't give up and quit talking about it, I wheeled out on you. That was a crappy thing for me to do."

It was a step. A rather large one, actually. "Your apology is accepted." She turned her attention to her dream house again.

"May I see?"

She didn't look up. "Sure."

He entered the studio and wheeled down the length of it, rolling around the outer edge of her drafting table and stopping at her side. "A house..."

"My dream house," she said. "Someday I'll build it. Ideally, in the Hill Country."

He took a few seconds to look over the drawings she'd done that night. "Not bad."

She stuck out an elbow and poked him in the ribs. "Kissing up much?"

"I never kiss up when we're discussing architecture—what's this?" He bent closer. "A dog shower and grooming station?"

"I just thought of that. It's off the garage. Very convenient."

"Do you have a dog?"

"I intend to. Big dogs. Several—well, at least two. And a couple of cats, as well."

"Where's the cat grooming station?" He leaned her way—just enough that she felt his arm brush hers. She caught a hint of his scent, clean and earthy at once, a scent that stirred her, made her think of the night before, of what they'd done in his chair—and later, on the tangled sheets of her bed.

She looked at him then and saw that he was watching her, his gaze intent. All at once, the air between them felt electric, charged with promise. She said, with a slight huskiness creeping in, "Cats don't need one. They groom themselves."

He leaned a little closer. "I do like your dream house."

She only nodded. And it came to her that from now on, whenever she imagined her dream house, it would be with him in it.

And that was just beyond depressing. If it didn't work out with him—and it most likely wouldn't—she would have to dream up some other house to build for the man who *could* love her, and the children they would have together.

Really, she was carrying this whole thing between them too far—and too fast.

His eyes had changed. They were suddenly sad. And a million miles away. "It looks like a great place to raise your children."

"Well, yes. That's the dream…."

He caught her hand, brushed his lips against her knuckles. She felt that light kiss so deeply, in the core of herself.

Oh, I am going down, she thought.

Going down and fading fast. Just the touch of his lips against her skin and she was done for, finished, gone.

How could she have let this happen?

He was so not the man she'd imagined herself falling

for. She'd always known that the man for her would be openhearted. And trusting. Someone kind and not cruel. Someone who would tell her all his secrets, someone who could love her without holding his deepest heart away from her.

Someone as different from the man beside her as day was from night.

And then, in a torn voice, he said, "I had…a child, Abilene. A little boy who died. His name was Elias."

Chapter Eleven

Abilene sat very still in her chair, her hand held in his.

He was ready, at last—ready to tell her about Elias. It hardly seemed possible, that this precious moment had finally come.

She forgot all about that other man, her ideal man. The one who loved her unconditionally, the one who never spoke harshly, who was always understanding.

Right now, there was only Donovan. He filled up her heart, banished her doubts.

It meant so much, proved so much. About how far they had come, with each other, *toward* each other.

Donovan said, "Elias was four when his mother, Julie, died."

She let out a low cry. "Oh, Donovan. His mom died, too?"

He gazed at her steadily. "That's right."

She asked, softly, "You were married then, you and... Julie?"

He shook his head. "We were together, for a while. But it didn't last long."

It seemed important, then, to tell him what she already knew. "That day I went to lunch with Luisa...?"

He made a knowing sound. "She told you about Elias." At her nod, he added, "I was afraid she might."

"Don't get the wrong idea. It wasn't a gossip session, I promise you. Luisa respects your privacy and your feelings."

"I know she does."

"She mentioned Elias, but only because she assumed that I already knew about him. When she found out I didn't, she wouldn't say much more. She said I should ask you."

"But you didn't." Donovan spoke gently, a simple statement of fact.

Abilene admitted, "I've been waiting, for you to tell me yourself, when you were ready. It seemed somehow wrong, for me to be the one to bring it up."

He almost smiled. "You rarely hesitate to say what's on your mind."

"True. And I did want to ask you about him, about Elias. About what he was like, and yes, how you lost him. But somehow, it never felt like the right time. I didn't want to ambush you with something like that. And I knew it had to be a really rough subject for you."

"Yeah." His eyes were more gray than blue right then, a ghostly gray. And his face, too, seemed worn. Haggard. "It is a rough subject."

"Luisa did say there used to be pictures of Elias, in the music room and the front room."

"I had all his pictures moved to my own rooms,

months ago, when I got back from the first series of surgeries after the fall. So no one would ask me about him—which was seriously faulty reasoning, if you think about it." His voice took on a derisive edge. He was mocking himself.

She understood. "Who was around to ask you?"

"Exactly. By then, I allowed no one inside this house but Ben and Anton and Olga. And I'd already told them in no uncertain terms that they were never again to mention Elias. And they didn't. It was part of their job description, not to push me, never to challenge me, not to mention my son. I had everything under control, I thought." The shadows in his eyes lightened a little as he gazed at her, and a hint of a smile came and went. "And then you came along…."

She squeezed his hand. "Tell me about Julie. Tell me… the rest."

"Julie…" His almost-smile appeared again, like the edge of the sun from behind a dark cloud. "She was a good woman. Straight ahead, you know? Honest. After it was over between us, when she found out she was pregnant, she told me right away. I asked her to marry me. She said no, that we didn't love each other that way and marriage between us wouldn't last. But she did want the baby. I had money by then. And Julie was an artist, a struggling one. She was barely getting by. So I agreed to pay enough child support that she wouldn't have to work and she could be a full-time mom."

"That was good of you."

He chuckled. "No. It was convenient for me. And it worked for Julie, too. She was devoted to Elias and happy to be able to be with him, to raise him without the constant pressure of having to make ends meet. Everybody won—Elias, Julie. And me. I had no interest in being a real dad. Not until Julie died out of nowhere, of a stroke, of all things. She had no family. What could I do?"

"You took your son to live with you."

"I didn't see a choice in the matter, and that's the hard truth."

"So it was a big change for you."

"I dreaded it, to be honest, having a kid around. I worked all over the world. And when I wasn't working, there were mountains I wanted to climb. If Julie's parents had still been alive, I would have turned Elias over to them in a heartbeat. Or to my mother. But as you know, she was gone, too."

Abilene searched his face. "You're being way too hard on yourself, you know that?"

"No. I'm just telling you the way it was. The way *I* was. That first year, after we lost Julie, that was rough. Elias suffered, missing his mom. But he was a sunny-natured guy at heart. A miracle of a kid, really. From the first, clutching that beat-up Elmo doll he carried everywhere with him, he was following me around. He was looking up at me with those trusting eyes, asking me questions." Donovan smiled, but his own eyes were suspiciously moist. He shook his head. "Elias never stopped with the questions. And as the months went by, I found I was only too happy to come up with the answers he needed, only too happy to be a real dad. He was so curious. And as he got over the loss of his mom, he didn't have to carry his stuffed Elmo around everywhere. He became…fearless. I loved that about him. I took him with me, when I was working. I hired a tutor. And a nanny, to go with us. We lived in San Francisco and Austin. And then in Lake Tahoe…." Donovan drew in a slow, shaky breath.

Abilene waited. She sensed the worst was coming.

And it was. "That was where it happened, in Lake

Tahoe." Donovan let go of her fingers then. He sank back into his wheelchair and gripped the wheels in either hand. "I had rented a vacation cabin there. The driveway was impossibly steep—and remember how I mentioned that Elias was fearless?"

"I remember."

"Six years old, and he loved nothing so much as to ride his Big Wheel down the steepest hill he could find—the driveway. And then he graduated to his first two-wheeler. That really freaked the nanny out, but I watched him and he was a natural athlete, lightning reflexes, great balance. I told her to back off, that Elias knew what he was doing, that he had sense as well as good reflexes—plus, she always made him wear his helmet. He would be fine. At first, she thought I was crazy. But then, after she watched him go flying down that hill a few times, she agreed with me. He was having a ball and he was perfectly safe."

A chill ran along the surface of her skin. "But he wasn't?"

Donovan shut his eyes, tight, as if he saw the worst all over again, and only wanted to block out the memory, erase it from his sight. "Elias rode that new two-wheeler down the driveway countless times without a scratch. And then there was the last time. The bike hit a rock—or so the medical examiner determined later. It was one of those freak things, out of nowhere. Must have caught him off-guard. Elias fell. He never wanted to wear his helmet. That time, apparently, he had it on to appease the nanny, but left the clasp undone. The helmet flew off. He hit his head. I found him at the bottom of the driveway. Just lying there. His eyes were open. He was gone, I knew it. But he seemed to be staring up at the pines, at the blue sky overhead...."

"Oh, Donovan." The words were useless, but she couldn't help it. She said them anyway. "I'm so sorry...."

After a moment, he looked at her. His face was so pale, suddenly. Pale as a man lying in his own coffin. As if he was the one who had died.

And maybe, in essence, he had.

"I didn't protect him," Donovan said. "He died because I loved his fearlessness. I ate it up, that he was such a bold little guy, that nothing got him down. I...didn't watch out for him."

She ached to argue, to insist that you can't possibly watch a child every moment of every day, that terrible things can happen, with no one to blame. But she had no doubt he'd heard all that before. And if Elias had been her child, such consolations, however true, wouldn't help in the least.

A father needed to protect his children. And if he failed at that, for whatever reason, nothing anyone could say would make the guilt and pain go away.

"The children's center?" she asked in a whisper.

He swallowed. Hard. "Yeah. The idea for the center was a lot about Elias. My son was gone, but I hoped that maybe, if I could help someone else's child to have a better start in life, it would mean something, somehow. It would make up, at least a little, for the life Elias was never going to have."

"Oh, Donovan, yes. It's a good thing, what you're doing, an important thing. The center *will* mean a lot to children who need it." The words were totally inadequate, but she offered them anyway, in a vain attempt to draw him back to her, to the world of the living.

"I thought I was over it." His voice was no more than a rough husk of sound. "I thought I had made my peace with Elias's death. For a year or so, I grieved. And then

I told myself I needed to let it go—let *him* go—to get on with my life."

"But you weren't over it. Not really."

He shook his head. "It all came back, after the accident, like some dangerous animal I had locked in a room and told myself I was safe, protected from. That animal got out. During those three days alone in that ice cave, that animal came after me. At first, I fought it. I told myself I could make it, I was going to be okay. But that, the fighting, the holding on, it didn't last long. Then I was wondering if I was going to die, and then I was *certain* that I would. I was making a kind of peace with death, an agreement. Death and I came to an understanding. We both knew it was time for me to go." He stared off into the far corner of the long room, past the shadowed open door down at the other end. And he was lost to her at that moment, lost to the world, gone from his own life.

She reached for him, touched his face. His skin felt cool, bloodless. "Donovan." She urged him to turn to her. "Look at me. Please..."

He did turn his face her way. But his eyes were empty. He said, "I thought about Elias a lot during those three days. I thought of the life he would never have, of the complete wrongness of that. By the end, before they found me, I was talking to him, to Elias. It seemed I could see his face. I could hear his voice, calling me, asking questions, asking where I was, why I had left him alone. And I started thinking it was good, right, that I should die and be with him. I knew I was *ready* to die. I wanted it. To die."

He seemed a million miles away from her then, back on that mountain, in unbearable pain, with only his lost son for company.

She feared for him, truly. And she hated herself a little.

For pushing him so hard, for challenging him, constantly, to open up to her, to face his demons.

What did she know, really, about all he had suffered, about how he might have managed to deal with the worst kind of loss a parent can ever know?

What right did she have, to rip away his protections, to drag him back to the world again? She could see a deeper truth now, one her own youth and optimism had blinded her to. She could see at last, that in his isolation and silence, he had found a kind of peace.

But then she had come and stolen his peace away, all the while telling herself it was for his own good.

His own good.

What did she know about what was good for him?

Desperation seized her. She found herself pleading with him. "But Donovan—Donovan, please. You didn't die. You made it back."

He only went on staring at her through those blank eyes. "Not really. My body was rescued, I went on breathing. But for all intents and purposes, I was dead...."

It was too much. He seemed so far away now, gone somewhere inside his own mind, into a cold and lifeless place where she would never be able to reach him. She couldn't bear it.

She clambered up out of her seat and reached for him, wrapping both arms around his broad shoulders, from the side, bending across his wheelchair. It was awkward, trying to hold him like that. And it wasn't enough, either. She couldn't hold him tight enough.

So she eased one foot up and over him, sliding it between his white-knuckled grip on the wheel and the crook of his elbow. He only sat there, still as a living statue, as she squirmed to get her other leg into the space between his arm and his torso.

Finally, she managed it. She straddled him as she had the night before—only then, it had been for their mutual pleasure.

Now, it was for comfort. Comfort for him.

And for herself, too.

It was the only way she had left to try and reach him, to make him come back to her from whatever dark place he had gone.

She wrapped her arms around him and she buried her head against his neck. She held on tight, so very tight....

At first, it was no good. She was holding on all by herself. And that was unbearable, that he just sat there, unmoving, like the dead man he'd claimed he already was.

She held on tighter, she pressed her lips to the cool flesh of his neck, she whispered his name, over and over again.

And slowly, so slowly, his arms relaxed their steely grip on the wheels. He lowered his head a little, enough that she felt the soft kiss of his breath, stirring her hair.

He said, so softly she almost didn't hear the word, "Abilene..." And then those powerful arms came around her. He was holding her as tightly as she held on to him.

And she was whispering, frantically, "It's not true—you know it's not. You're here, with me. You're okay and you have to go on now. You have to learn to go on...."

He pressed his lips to her temple, a fervent caress. And then he was cradling her face between his two hands, urging her to lift her head, to look at him.

And she did look—and it *was* okay. He was all right. The color was back in his cheeks, and his eyes were focused, alive. He was there, in the studio, in the *world*, with her again.

She took his mouth—a hard, quick kiss. A claiming kiss. Once, and then a second time. "Oh, you scared me. You did. You really did…."

He eased her away from him enough that he could capture her gaze and hold it. "Okay," he said, firmly. Decisively.

She didn't get it, had no idea what he was telling her. "Okay, what?"

"Okay, you were right."

"Um. I was?"

"Sometimes I hate it, you know? How right you are?"

"I have to tell you, Donovan. Sometimes I don't feel very right. Sometimes I feel like I haven't got a clue."

"Coulda fooled me."

"Yeah. Well, I put on a pretty good act, I guess, huh?"

He searched her face. And then he gave a low chuckle. "You have no idea what I'm talking about, do you?"

"Well…"

"Do you?"

She was busted. "I hate to admit it, but no. I don't."

"I'm saying you were right, tonight, at the dinner table. And after I wheeled out on you, after I went to my rooms to sulk, I stared at the portrait of Elias over the fireplace, and I thought about how I let him down the day he died, by not watching out for him closely enough, by being too damn proud of him to do what was good for him, to tell him it wasn't safe, tell him no. And stick by it."

It was futile to argue that point, she got that. But she couldn't just keep letting it go, either. "Oh, Donovan…"

She put up a hand between them, touched her fingers to his lips.

His gold brows drew together. "What?"

"Sometimes terrible things happen, no matter what you do to make sure that they don't."

He caught her fingers, eased them away. "I'm very well aware of that." The bitterness was there, in his tone, again—and in his eyes. "And it doesn't help to know that, doesn't help when people say it. It doesn't help in the least."

She lowered her head in surrender. "No," she said quietly. "I can see that it doesn't." She reminded herself—again—that nothing she could say was going to make him stop blaming himself. He had to come to forgiving himself in his own way, in his own time.

He touched her chin, so gently. When she looked up, the anger was gone from his face. He spoke tenderly. "What I'm trying to tell you is that I get it. I understand. I made a commitment when I offered the fellowship for the children's center, and that commitment was not only to the children who need the center, not only to the Foundation, not only to you. It was also to Elias. For his sake most of all, I have to follow through. If I don't, I'll be letting him down all over again."

Her breath got all tangled up in her throat and her heart beat faster, with pure joy. It was happening. He'd seen what he needed to do at last.

And he'd decided to go for it.

He said, "You were right, Abilene, as you are way too much of the time. I'll be going to San Antonio with you, after all."

Chapter Twelve

He took her to his rooms. She saw the pictures of Elias, at last.

"Oh, I wish I could have known him," she said.

"He would have liked you." Donovan's voice was rough with feeling. He held out his hand to her.

She went to him. She kissed him. They undressed each other slowly and went to bed.

They didn't get to sleep until very late. But they were up at dawn, nonetheless.

Now that he'd made the decision to go, Donovan was wasting no time about it. He wanted to be in San Antonio, ready to work, within the week.

Sunday morning, he started surfing the internet, looking for a place he might stay for an indefinite period, somewhere with good wheelchair access. A few hotels offered what he needed. But he was hoping he could find a house to rent. After a couple of hours of looking, he'd come up with zip.

Abilene suggested, "You should call Dax. He and Zoe have plenty of room."

Donovan hesitated. He didn't want to put them out. It seemed presumptuous. They'd invited him to visit, not to move in on them while he worked.

Abilene marched down the length of the studio to his desk, grabbed the phone and shoved it at him. "They would love to have you. They have plenty of room. Their house is so big, you could move in there permanently. Unless they wanted to see you, they would never even realize you were there."

He slanted her a put-upon look. "Have I told you that you are one extremely annoying and pushy woman?"

"You have. Frequently. Make the call."

He took the phone she held under his nose and dialed Dax's number.

Dax said Donovan was welcome to live at his place, for as long as he wanted to stay. He and Zoe would be gone next week, when Donovan arrived. They traveled a lot, gathering material for his magazine. But he had live-in staff who would have Donovan's rooms ready and waiting for him.

Donovan thanked him, and explained what he needed in terms of access for his wheelchair. And Dax promised it was all workable. There was a suite on the main floor that should be ideal. Meals would be available at Donovan's convenience, since the cook lived in.

So it was settled. Donovan would stay with the Girards. Abilene had her condo waiting for her—though she wouldn't mind at all if she ended up spending her nights at her sister's, in Donovan's rooms.

Monday, when Helen came to work, Donovan asked

her to accompany them to San Antonio. But she didn't want to leave her husband alone in Chula Mesa. So he had her call a San Antonio temp agency. They would send someone to Dax's as soon as Donovan got settled in. Also, Helen found trainers and a massage therapist in San Antonio who would work with Donovan while he was there.

Anton and Olga would remain in West Texas to take care of the house. And Helen would come in three times a week to deal with correspondence and anything else that might need her attention while Donovan was away.

As the week went by, Donovan spent a lot of time on the phone with the Foundation people. They were thrilled to learn that he and his protégé would be showing up very soon now. There were conference calls with Ruth Gilman and Doug Lito at the Johnson Wallace Group and with the builder, Sam Duncan of SA Custom Contracting. The site, chosen over a year before, was ready and waiting. The formal groundbreaking ceremony would be going forward on March first, as planned.

Abilene spent her days working feverishly to be ready to go—and her nights in Donovan's bed. She loved the picture of Elias in his sailor suit and talked Donovan into moving it back out to the main living area.

Wednesday night, at dinner, he told Olga to take the portrait out of his sitting room and put it back where it belonged, over the front room fireplace.

Tears welled in Olga's eyes. "Yes. Of course. An excellent decision. He was the sweetest boy. And we miss him, so much."

Thursday night, Luisa came to dinner. She told Donovan how happy it made her, to see that he'd put Elias's picture back in the front room.

"Blame Abilene," he said. "She made me do it." And

he sent Abilene a look that melted her midsection and made her toes curl inside her high-heeled shoes.

Luisa wanted them to come to the cantina one more time before they left for San Antonio.

So Friday night, they drove out to the roadhouse. They had margaritas and played pool—and Donovan got his butt kicked again by that tall, tattooed blonde. They were back at the house before midnight and went together to Donovan's rooms, where they made slow, tender love and fell asleep in each other's arms.

Abilene woke Saturday morning in Donovan's bed. She watched him sleeping and found herself wishing she could wake up beside him every morning, for the rest of her life.

She loved him—was *in* love with him. And for the past few busy days, she'd been trying to figure out how to tell him. It seemed such a simple thing. She ought to just say it. *I love you, Donovan.*

But she didn't. Somehow, the moment never quite seemed right.

Strange, really. She'd always been the kind who said exactly what was on her mind.

But on this whole I-love-you thing, well, she kept hesitating, kept putting it off. She didn't want to push him. Not about something so important as love.

Not about something as far-reaching as the possibility of forever.

On the pillow beside her, he opened his eyes.

She thought, *I love you.* But all she said was, "Good morning."

Donovan met her shining eyes and knew what he had to do. But somehow, he just couldn't bring himself to do it.

What he had with her, he'd never had with any woman—that sense that she knew him, knew who he really was. That she accepted him, completely, and yet still expected him to be the best he could possibly be.

He felt the same way about her. He *knew* her in the deepest way. He accepted her as the brilliant, pushy, tenderhearted woman she was. And he wanted the best for her. He wanted her to have the chance to make all her dreams come true.

She couldn't do that with him. He didn't share her dreams. He couldn't. Not anymore. He kept thinking about that fantasy house of hers—her dream house—about the husband and children she wanted to build it for. He was never going to be the husband in that house, or the father of those children.

He reached out and brushed the back of his hand along the velvety curve of her cheek, thinking that he somehow had to find a way to make her understand why he had to leave her.

Not now, though.

Not yet…

So he thought, *I have to leave you.* But all he said was, "Good morning."

Later that day, Abilene packed up her car. She would leave, on her own, early Sunday morning.

Donovan would fly to San Antonio on Monday. He'd offered to ride with Abilene, to keep her company. But they both knew an eight-hour car ride would be uncomfortable for him. In the end, he'd admitted it was probably wiser for him to fly. Helen had made arrangements for a van with a wheelchair lift to be available at the San Antonio airport, so he would have the use of a car when he got there.

That night, late, it rained. A real gulley-washer. Abilene heard the soft, insistent roar of it outside and woke. Beside her, Donovan slept on.

Slowly, with care, so as not to wake him, she rose from the bed, grabbed her robe from a nearby chair and slipped it on. Barefoot, she padded into his sitting room, where she gazed out at the torrent. It was coming down so hard it made the water in the pool churn and ran in little rivers along the courtyard pathways. Lightning brightened the sky and thunder boomed somewhere in the distance.

She stood there at the glass door for several minutes, watching the rain come down and the lightning flash, listening to the rumbles of thunder.

"Looks pretty wild out there," Donovan said from behind her.

She turned to him. "I didn't mean to wake you."

"You didn't. The thunder did." His white teeth flashed with his smile. In the darkness, his eyes were almost black. He'd pulled on sweats before he wheeled in to join her.

She went to him, bent to kiss him. He reached for her and pulled her down across his lap. She curved against him, her legs over one wheel, an arm around his neck, her head tucked beneath his chin.

He kissed the top of her head. "Ready for the big drive tomorrow?"

"All packed." She nuzzled his throat, breathed in the clean scent of his skin, thought how she hated to be apart from him, even just for a day.

Lightning flashed again. The room brightened.

She lifted her head and met his eyes as the room darkened once more and the thunder rolled off across the desert floor. "It almost feels unreal, that we're leaving.

Five weeks out here, and it's as if I've been here, with you, forever."

"Five weeks," he echoed. "And I spent most of it making your life as miserable as possible."

"The past week is the one that counts."

He held her gaze. "They all count. You know that." And then he guided her head down to his shoulder again. "It will be good, though, won't it? To see your family, to go home...?"

"Um-hm." *I love you.* She thought the words. But she didn't say them.

Five weeks, she had known him. Five weeks was nothing. Even if it did kind of feel like forever.

And as he'd just said, only in the past week had they truly found each other.

They both needed more time.

At least a little more.

And a chance to be together out in the real world. His house was beautiful and so comfortable and lately, it had started to feel like her home, somehow. But it was a place apart, where the world outside could not intrude.

San Antonio would be the proof of what they had together. He would meet her family. And the work on the children's center would proceed beyond just the two of them.

Yes. It was good, that they were going.

And this strange feeling she had, the one she kept denying. The feeling that his going with her to San Antonio was an end instead of the beginning...

That would pass, like the lightning and the thunder, like a sudden midnight storm across the wide-open desert.

He smoothed her hair. "Back to bed?"

She lifted her head again, touched her lips to his.

"Please." And then she shifted on his lap, turning to face front, bringing her legs down over his, out of the way of the wheels.

He rolled them both in a circle and back to the other room.

The next morning, she said goodbye to Anton and Olga and thanked them for everything.

Olga hugged her and whispered to her to come back soon.

"I will," she promised.

Donovan went with her down to the garage. She kissed him and told him she would see him tomorrow.

He said, "Call me when you get there?"

She promised that she would.

And then she got into her Prius and headed for home.

The drive was every bit as long and tedious as she remembered. But she finally arrived. At a little after five that afternoon, she lugged her suitcases into her condo.

Her place was pretty much as she'd left it—including the Christmas tree in the window and the fat red candles in festive holders on the mantel. When the summons had come from Donovan the day after New Year's, she'd had no time to put away her holiday decorations.

She called Donovan's cell.

He answered on the first ring. "You made it." The sound of his voice warmed her, banished all her strange, persistent doubts. "I've been waiting for you to call…."

She said, "It's crazy. We've been apart for eight hours and fifteen minutes. And I miss you so much."

He said nothing.

Her doubts came flooding back, drowning her. "Donovan?"

And then he confessed gruffly, "Yeah. I miss you, too."

She told herself she was being so silly—and definitely paranoid. And she asked, "Tomorrow?"

He confirmed it. "Tomorrow."

"I could come to the airport and meet you…."

"No. I'll have the van waiting. There's no point."

She wanted to argue that of course there was a point. To see him. To be with him as soon as she possibly could.

But she didn't argue. She told herself to get over this burning need to be near him constantly. Just because she loved him didn't mean she had to turn into some wimpy clinging vine.

She answered with determined cheerfulness. "Then I'll be waiting at Zoe and Dax's."

He said he would see her then. They said goodbye.

She felt let down and lonely—which was totally self-indulgent. So she ordered a pizza and called her mom. Aleta didn't answer the phone at home, so she tried the family ranch, Bravo Ridge, where her mom and dad usually went for Sunday dinner.

Mercy, her sister-in-law, answered. "Everyone's here," she said. "Why don't you come on out?"

"I'd love to, but I've been driving all day and my place is still decorated for Christmas. I need to take down all this holiday stuff."

"Next Sunday then. Family dinner here, as always. Think about it."

"I will. Thanks. Is Mom there?"

"Right here…"

Her mother came on the line. "You're home?"

"Yep. Safe and well."

"How about lunch, tomorrow?"

"Oh, I'd love to. But I can't. Donovan is coming in around noon and I—"

"Honey." Her mother's voice was full of love and patience. "I understand. Of course, you'll want to see that he's all settled at Zoe's."

"Yes. Especially, you know, since Zoe and Dax are out of town."

"Sweetheart, I agree. You should be there to greet him."

"Thanks. For understanding."

"I do want to meet him soon."

"Yes. Absolutely. Tomorrow will be impossible, though, and probably the rest of the week. We have meetings and more meetings."

"How about next Sunday? You can both come out here, to the ranch, for dinner."

She pictured the wide white steps up to the deep front verandah of the Greek Revival-style ranch house. Wheelchair accessible, it wasn't. "Can I get back to you?"

"That will be fine. And call me any time you think you might be able to slip away for a bit, just the two of us."

"I will. I love you."

"Love you, too…"

They said goodbye.

The pizza came. After she'd devoured three big slices, Abilene got busy. She unpacked and went through the pile of junk mail that her neighbor had picked up for her. The houseplants didn't need watering. The same neighbor had kept an eye on them.

But the Christmas stuff really did have to go. She took it all down and packed everything away.

By the time she was done, it was after ten. She filled the tub and soaked for half an hour, easing away the kinks from those long hours on the road. And then, finally, she crawled into bed, where she lay wide awake half the night.

She missed the warmth of Donovan beside her, missed the soft, even sound of his breathing as he slept.

And she kept feeling that something was not right.

Which was silly, she reminded herself over and over. Everything was fine. Donovan would join her tomorrow. And on Tuesday, the next phase of work on the children's center would begin.

In the morning, she packed a suitcase and went to Zoe and Dax's house, which was just outside of San Antonio, in an exclusive gated community.

She gave her name at the front gate and then again at the gate to the Girard estate. In the cavern of a garage, she parked her little car between a Bentley and an Aston Martin, and left her suitcase in the trunk to bring in later.

Dax and Zoe's house was three stories and sixteen thousand square feet of pure luxury, the furnishings mostly modern, but with a lot of the interesting accent pieces that Dax had picked up on his travels all over the world.

The housekeeper welcomed her and showed her to Donovan's rooms, which were spacious and comfortable. Both the bedroom and the sitting area had views of the back grounds and the pool.

Abilene had been to the house twice before, during the holidays, after her sister and Dax had decided to get married. On the first visit, Zoe had given her a full tour, so she knew her way around inside and out.

Donovan had had his luggage sent ahead. The housekeeper, Pauline, led the way to the walk-in closet, where his shoes were arrayed on handsome wooden racks and everything else was either waiting on hangers or neatly folded and put away in drawers.

Abilene thanked Pauline and said that yes, she would ring if she needed anything. The housekeeper left her.

By then, it was ten-thirty. Donovan's plane wasn't due to land for half an hour. It could be a couple of hours before he arrived at the house.

She went outside and strolled around the grounds for a while. Back inside, she stopped at the restaurant-size kitchen, where the cook gave her coffee and a warm chocolate croissant.

Her phone chimed as she was wandering back to Donovan's rooms. A text.

It was from Donovan. Just landed. No probs. C U soon.

She grinned like an idiot and texted back, Here. W8ing. She longed to add Luv U, but she stopped her eager thumbs just in time. She hit Send, fast, before she could change her mind again and do it anyway.

It was too early, she reminded herself for the ten-thousandth time. And besides, it would be just too tacky, to declare her love via text message. Too tacky. Too soon.

He answered with a simple, Gr8.

And that was that.

Danger averted. Love not so much as mentioned or in any way alluded to.

In Donovan's bedroom, she stood at the window and looked out at the pool and tried to figure out why she kept feeling so disconnected, so…wrong.

When no answer came to her, she went to the bed and kicked off her shoes and stretched out on her back.

The room was quiet and she was pretty tired, since she'd barely slept the night before.

She closed her eyes, let out a slow sigh. Really, a half-hour nap might be just what she needed….

Dax's housekeeper was waiting in the garage when Donovan pulled the van in.

She indicated the empty space a few slots away from Abilene's dusty Prius, and then waited some more as he unhooked his chair and wheeled to the lift and down.

"I'm Pauline. Welcome," she said, once he'd rolled off the lift and locked up the van.

Pauline led him out of the garage, down a wide hallway and up a short ramp, into another hallway somewhere in the back half of Dax's enormous house. She showed him the kitchen before she took him to his rooms. "Help yourself to anything you might like," she said.

"Thanks." The door in there, like every door he'd seen so far, was more than wide enough to wheel through. The doorways matched the house; everything on a grand scale.

"Abilene is in your rooms," Pauline said as they started down another wide hallway with a twelve-foot ceiling and a silver-flecked ivory granite floor.

Abilene. He'd been kind of wondering why she hadn't come out to meet him. He was anxious to see her. Ridiculously so.

"I checked on her a few minutes ago," said the housekeeper. "She's napping. I hated to wake her…."

Napping. He should have known. She worked so hard. And she'd spent all day yesterday on the road.

"Here we are," said the housekeeper, stopping at a half-open door. "Your suitcases arrived safely and I've had everything put away."

"Thank you."

"Is there anything in the vehicle that you'd like me to have brought in to you?"

"There's a briefcase and a small overnight bag. I'll get them later."

"If you need anything, just pick up the phone. House line is blue, to reach me. The green button is the kitchen."

He thanked her again.

She nodded and left him alone at last.

He went in, stopping to shut the door and engage the privacy lock behind him. The sitting room was big and inviting, furnished with simple, expensive pieces, mostly in reds and tans.

But he didn't hang around in there. He went through the wide doorway to the bedroom.

And found what he was looking for.

She was sound asleep, her silky hair spread across the pillow and a peaceful expression on her fine-boned face. She wore canvas trousers and a slouchy sweater and she'd kicked off her flat-soled shoes. Her slender feet were bare, her pretty toenails painted the color of plums.

His sleeping princess from his own private fairy tale.

He went to her, drawn as if by a magnet. When he got to the side of the bed, he shucked off his shoes, locked his wheels and, with great care, pressed his palms to the mattress beside her and levered himself out of the chair.

She opened her eyes as he lowered himself to a sitting position next to her. "Donovan. You're here." Her face lit up as if from within.

And he couldn't help himself. His heart melted.

He saw in her eyes what it could be, with them. He

was in it, he lived it—a whole, rich, wonderful life, at her side.

The fine work they would do. The bright, bold, unbounded happiness they would share.

The love they would make.

The troubles they would overcome, the dark times that would always, inevitably, give way to light….

No, it wasn't going to happen. But at that moment, in that large, well-appointed room, with the bright winter-afternoon sunlight streaming in across the tan cover of the bed, picking up gold highlights in her dark-toffee hair, he pretended that it would.

She reached for him, sighing welcome.

And he went down to her, ignoring the twinges in his messed-up legs as he hauled them up onto the mattress and then out as straight as they would go. With effort, he rolled to his side, facing her, and he gathered her into him, covering her soft mouth with his own.

They both groaned at the contact. Instantly, she opened for him. He speared his tongue inside, where it was wet and hot and oh, so sweet. She sucked on it, ran her own tongue around it, teasing him, laughing a little, deep in her throat, a rough purr of sound that vibrated into the core of him.

Already, he was hard, aching to be inside her.

And she was slipping her hand down between them, cupping him with another eager moan, pressing the length of him, caressing him as her body rocked against him, making him harder still.

"The door?" she whispered against his lips.

"Locked it."

"Ah." She went on kissing him—deep, wet, sucking kisses. Endless kisses.

Her nimble fingers worked at his fly. She had his

zipper down in an instant, and she was slipping that slim, clever hand of hers under the waistband of his boxer briefs.

She encircled him. He groaned into her mouth as she pushed at him, urging him over to lie on his back.

He went, not even aware by then of his legs, of the twinges and twitches, the pain that was there, whenever he moved them. Right now, he felt a different ache. A good ache, dark and sweet, rolling through him in hungry waves.

Whatever she wanted from him, she could have. He was hers to command.

She left him—just long enough to get out of her trousers and little silk panties. And then she was back, pushing at his clothes enough to clear the way, easing his cell and his keys from his pockets, setting them on the nightstand, out of her way.

He shut his eyes, swept away by the sheer pleasure her touch always brought. And when he looked again, she was above him, straddling him, up on her knees, gazing down at him, her eyes soft and shining, her mouth curving in a sensual smile.

Slowly, by aching degrees, she lowered her body onto his, taking him within her, so deep.

All the way.

He made some absurd, lost groaning sound. And she laughed, low. Huskily. She knew her power over him. It was absolute. She bent down to him, kissed him.

But only briefly, a brushing touch of her lips to his, her hair falling forward around them like a veil of silk. When he tried to follow, lifting his head off the pillows to keep from losing the tenuous connection of that kiss, she laughed again.

And she rose up once more, pushing her hips down

on him, locking her body to his. And she took that big sweater she wore and ripped it off, tossing it away, her beautiful hair crackling with static, lifting as she pulled the sweater over her head, then falling in a wild tumble to her shoulders again.

Her bra was nothing more than a bit of pink lace.

He reached up, curved his fingers around one lacy cup, feeling the warmth and fullness of the sweet flesh beneath. "Take it off." He moaned the words.

She reached behind her, undid the clasp and let it drop down her arms. He took it from her, rumpled the lace in his hand, brought it to his face, breathed in the tempting apple and watermelon scent that clung to it—and then he dropped it over the side of the bed.

He reached for her. She came down to him, fusing her mouth to his, kissing him so deeply now. He cradled her breasts, stroked her back and ran his hands up over her shoulders, into the lush silk of her hair.

She moved on him, deep strokes, slow and hot and overwhelming. He was lost—lost in her—never, ever wanting to be found.

When the finish came, she stilled above him. He wrapped her tighter in his arms, knew a breath-held wonder as they rose together.

And then the long, sweet pulse of slow release.

Not much later, his cell rang.

"Don't answer that," she commanded.

But then she allowed him to look at the display, at least.

"It's Jessica Nevis, with the Foundation."

She sighed. "Go ahead."

He spoke to Jessica, confirmed that they would meet tomorrow morning, at nine.

And he no sooner hung up, than Ruth Gilman's assistant called, from Johnson Wallace, just confirming, for tomorrow. Ruth would be there and Doug, as well, when they met with the Foundation people at nine.

And after Ruth's assistant, the builder called, too.

When he finally put the cell back on the nightstand and pulled Abilene close again, she asked, "Where is that temporary assistant when you need her?"

"That reminds me—I need to call the temp agency. There's not going to be any time to deal with the temp until Wednesday, at the earliest." He tried to reach for the phone again.

She caught his hand and kissed it. "Wait. Just for a few minutes."

He gave in and settled back on the pillow again, with her cradled close to his side.

"I have a confession." She pressed her lips to the side of his neck, whispered, "I brought a suitcase."

"What?" He pretended to grumble. "You're moving in on me?"

"Yes, I am." She snuggled in closer. "Don't try to escape."

"On these legs? I don't think so." He caught her mouth. They shared a kiss, and then she curled against his shoulder with a sigh.

Idly, he ran his hand down the silky skin of her arm. She felt good in his arms. As if she belonged there.

And really, she did. At least for the next month.

He'd thought long and hard about when to end it, about whether or not he should get it out there now, have a long talk with her, remind her of what he'd told her that day he wheeled in on her in the shower, that love and forever were not an option.

But then again, when they had that talk, knowing her,

there was going to be trouble. She was going to be really angry with him. He got that. He accepted that.

And right now, he didn't want her distracted from the job they needed to do together, didn't want her so furious with him that it got in the way for her. When he left her, he wanted her all set up as the supervising architect on the project—with the Foundation, with Johnson Wallace, with the builder, with all of them.

She had given him so much and he wanted her future assured. It was the least he could leave her with.

Or so he told himself.

At the same time, somewhere in his guilty heart, he knew he was a liar. The worst kind of liar, the kind who lied to himself.

The real problem was that he wanted more time with her. They'd only just found each other. And he simply couldn't bear to let her go.

Not so soon. Not quite yet.

Chapter Thirteen

The Foundation people were thrilled with the design. They gave their full approval to proceed.

During the presentation, Donovan deferred to Abilene. He made sure they all knew that it was her dedication and talent that had made the design come together. He explained that she would be taking the position of lead architect as they moved toward construction, though of course, he would be available whenever he was needed.

Ruth Gilman, who was in her early fifties, slim and impeccably dressed, with short strawberry-blond hair, remembered meeting Abilene at some charity function or other. The two of them really seemed to hit it off. Donovan had been sure they would. Ruth had always liked to encourage up-and-coming architects, especially female ones.

They all went to lunch to celebrate—Donovan and

Abilene, Ruth Gilman, Doug Lito and Jessica Nevis. Jessica left them after the meal. They moved on to the Johnson Wallace offices, where they met with the builder.

Around four, Jessica and a couple of others from the Foundation joined them. They went over everything, fine-tuning the basic design, working into the evening, and calling it quits around seven.

Donovan was tired when they got back to Dax's; his legs ached and twitched. But it hadn't been as difficult as he'd expected, to spend a whole day working from his wheelchair, dealing with a lot of people, never getting a break to go work out the kinks in the gym.

Still, he told Abilene he was exhausted. And that his legs bothered him more than they actually did.

And when she got on him for giving her all the credit with the Foundation people, he was able to convince her that she needed to accept the credit—and shoulder most of the work. He said he wasn't at the point where he could consistently spend whole days at Johnson Wallace, or at the construction site, for that matter.

She kissed him and said she would do her best.

And then she asked him to go with her to her family's ranch for Sunday dinner. She added, "That is, if you can bear the indignity of having one of my brothers carry you up the front steps." She looked adorably anxious, afraid he would be too proud to agree.

Meeting the parents. He shouldn't do that. It would be only another lie, another indication to her that he was thinking in terms of a future for them.

And it would have been so simple, just to mutter gruffly that he wasn't comfortable with having one of her brothers carrying him anywhere, just to let her think his pride was the problem.

But he looked in her beautiful, shining, hopeful face—and he couldn't do it, couldn't tell that particular lie.

"Life is full of indignities," he said, and gathered her close. "What's one more?"

They were hard at work again by 9:00 a.m. the next day, spending the morning at Johnson Wallace and the afternoon at the cleared construction site. For Donovan, that day was actually easier than the day before. He saw possibilities for himself now, in terms of his future and his work, possibilities that he hadn't seen before.

But again that night, he lied to Abilene. He made a big deal of his exhaustion and pain.

Thursday morning, he finally got to meet with his temporary assistant. The first task he set her was to find him another place to stay, one with wheelchair access. A house to rent, if possible.

It bothered him to be taking advantage of Dax's hospitality, mostly because Dax was married to Abilene's sister. It was bad enough that he was lying by omission to Abilene about their possible future. He shouldn't be mooching off her family at the same time.

The temp didn't disappoint him. That day, she found him a nice house in Olmos Park, one that had just become available as a sublet for two months while the owners—one of whom was a paraplegic—were out of the country.

He left Abilene happily working with Ruth at Johnson Wallace and went to see the place. It was one story, with ramps leading up to all the entrances. It had space he could use for an office, a small exercise room and a kitchen specially designed with lowered counters. He could cook his own meals there, from his wheelchair.

So he took it, paid for both months, though if everything went according to his plan, he would only need it until the first week of March. Then he had his assistant find him a part-time housekeeper.

That night, during dinner, just the two of them, at Dax's, he told Abilene about the house he'd rented and that he'd be moving there the next day.

She set down her fork. "I'm…surprised. I thought it was working out well for you, staying here."

"It is. It's great. But I don't feel right, taking advantage of Dax like this."

She sighed and fiddled with her water glass. His gut knotted and he was sure that she would argue. That she would ask too many questions and he would end up saying too much.

But in the end, she only picked up her fork again. "I get it. You like your own…space."

"That's it, exactly." Well, okay. It wasn't all of it. But she didn't need to know that. Not now. Right now, she needed to put her boundless energy where it mattered—on the work she was doing, on the center she would be helping to build. And on the future she was creating for herself.

She looked at him sideways. "Do I get to see this house you'll be staying at?"

"Absolutely."

"When?"

"I'm thinking tomorrow, for dinner."

"Do I get to…sleep over?"

"I hope you will."

She laughed then. "I'll bring my suitcase."

She did bring her suitcase.

She stayed with him Friday night, and Saturday, too. Sunday, they went out to Bravo Ridge, her family's ranch, where her brother Luke carried him up the wide front steps and he met her mom and dad and Luke's wife, Mercy, along with five other brothers, their wives and a few very cute children.

Over dinner, one of the wives, Irina, announced that she and Caleb, the fifth-born Bravo brother, were expecting a baby in August. Everyone jumped up, the men to clap a beaming Caleb on the back and the women to pull the serenely smiling Irina from her chair and pass her from one laughing, congratulatory hug to the next.

For Donovan, the moment was bittersweet. He envied Caleb. He envied all the Bravo men—whole and strong, married to women they obviously loved. Unafraid to be fathers, secure in the firm belief that they could protect their children and their women from harm.

Overall, though, Donovan enjoyed himself that day. They were good people, he thought. Abilene's mom, Aleta, was especially charming. He saw Abilene in her—in the way she tipped her head when she was listening, in the curve of her mouth when she smiled. And her father, Davis, was something of an architecture buff. He knew of the five-star hotel Donovan had designed in Dallas, and the headquarters for that office supplies conglomerate he'd built in Manhattan.

They all stayed well into the evening, playing pool in the game room and then returning to the dining room for a late dessert. At a little after eight, Luke carried him back down the front steps. Gabe, the second-born brother, brought his wheelchair down and set it up for him at the back of the van. Before he rolled onto the lift and in behind the wheel, he thanked them all.

Aleta bent close and hugged him and told him to come back any time.

"I liked them," he reassured Abilene, later, in bed.

She kissed him and whispered, "They liked you, too."

Monday was Valentine's Day. Donovan took Abilene to her favorite restaurant. They went home to his rented house and made slow, beautiful love. She fell asleep in his arms. He cradled her close and tried not to think about how fast each day was going by.

He wished he could hold back time, make it stand still. Just for a little while.

But time failed to cooperate. It flew by.

That Wednesday, Zoe and Dax returned, and the four of them had dinner together. Dax had always been a player, dating one gorgeous woman after another. But it was obvious that he'd found all the woman he needed in the six-months-pregnant Zoe, who had long red hair, a great sense of humor and a mind as sharp as Abilene's.

Later, the men retreated to Dax's study, where they drank very old Cognac and Dax tried to get him to talk about Abilene. But Donovan had a feeling that whatever he said would go right back to Zoe—and from Zoe, to Abilene.

So he was evasive. And Dax didn't push.

And that night, when they were alone, Abilene talked about how happy her sister seemed, how great it was that Zoe and Dax had found each other. He agreed.

She gazed at him expectantly. "A little like us, huh?"

Again, he lied by omission. He pulled her down into his lap, tipped her chin up and kissed her, ending a dangerous conversation before it could really get started.

Every evening, it seemed, there was someone new Abilene wanted him to meet. Friday night, he met Javier Cabrera, the builder Abilene admired so much. Javier was also the man whose estranged wife had once had an affair with Abilene's father—a brief liaison, which had resulted in Abilene's half sister, Elena.

Javier came to dinner at the rental house in Olmos Park. He was a compact, powerfully built man, with silver-shot black hair. He treated Abilene with honest affection and respect. Donovan felt drawn to him. There was loneliness in the older man's dark eyes, and wisdom, too. Javier said he was considering selling his business. That he didn't have the heart for his work anymore. That he was ready to retire.

As soon as the older man was out the door, Abilene turned to Donovan, tears in her eyes. "He seems even sadder than ever. I just want to grab him, you know? Grab him and shake him and tell him to go to his wife, go right away. To tell her he loves her and he forgives her for what she did all those years ago, to swear that all he wants is to get back together with her."

Donovan only shook his head. "Some things, a man has to figure out for himself."

Two fat tears overflowed the dam of her lower lids and trailed a gleaming path down her soft cheeks. "And some things, I guess, just can't be forgiven."

He reached for her hand then, and pulled her down to him. She curled into him as if she belonged there, in his arms. He wished for the impossible, that he would never have to let her go.

The weekend passed, a weekend they spent together, he and Abilene.

She had essentially moved in with him. He shouldn't have allowed that, shouldn't have indulged himself so completely with her. But he did it anyway.

Every night with her was a night to remember, a night to treasure. He was hoarding those nights, storing them up in his heart. When he no longer had her with him, at least he would have the memories of her.

And during the day, he'd established a schedule much like the one he'd kept when she came to his house in the desert. He checked in and out with Johnson Wallace and the builder, making himself available when necessary, but pushing Abilene to the fore.

It went well, though by the end of their second week in San Antonio, he did notice a certain watchfulness in Abilene. She asked him Tuesday evening if something was bothering him.

He lied and said there was nothing. After that, it seemed to him, she was quieter, less lively somehow.

Except when they went to bed.

In his arms, she came alive. She burned with a bright fire, taking the lead, driving him wild. He was only too happy to be consumed by the flames.

By the next week, the third week in February, the Foundation people, the Johnson Wallace team and the builder all seemed to have accepted that they were working with Abilene. That Wednesday night, again, she asked him if there was something wrong.

He denied it.

And then, both Thursday and Friday, he stayed away from Johnson Wallace, didn't even look in to see how the project was going. He knew he would hear from them if there was an issue and that Abilene could handle things without him hanging around.

He got no calls. No one seemed to notice his absence.

Or so he thought, until Friday night, when Abilene got home.

She came into the kitchen, dropped her big leather bag

on the chair by the door and said, "Okay. It's enough. We've got to talk about this."

Abilene waited, her pulse a roar in her ears, her stomach tied so tight, in painful knots, as Donovan lowered the heat under the sausage he was cooking and turned off the burner beneath the big pot he used for boiling pasta. He wheeled over to the sink to rinse and dry his hands.

Oh, she did not want to go here. She didn't want to confront him.

But really, they couldn't just keep on like this. Pretending everything was all right, playing house in this cute little place he'd rented.

Finally, he turned to her. His eyes were a cool, distant gray. "Talk about what?"

Talk about what? The words bounced around in her brain, and she wanted to fling them right back at him, *Talk about what? As if you don't know...*

Resolutely, she marched to the small breakfast table by the bow window, pulled out a chair and lowered herself into it. "Please." She gestured at the empty space across from her.

He didn't move, only suggested so gently, "Abilene, you don't have to do this."

A torn sound escaped her. "If I don't, then what?"

"Abilene..." His voice trailed off. He shook his head.

At that moment, she almost hated him. She *would* have hated him, if only she didn't love him so damn much.

She asked in a voice barely above a whisper, "Is it the groundbreaking ceremony? Is that the end? Is that when you're leaving me?"

He glanced away, which only made her more certain that it had to be the groundbreaking ceremony.

She pointed at the place across the table again, asked for the second time, "Please?"

And at last, he moved. He wheeled around the central island and took the space she'd indicated. When he stopped, he kept his hands at his wheels. As if, at any second, he would back and turn and roll out the kitchen door and away—from her, from this moment, from the words that needed to be said.

She folded her hands on the table. "I don't want to fight, Donovan. I just want to talk. To talk honestly."

His Adam's apple lurched as he swallowed. And he nodded. But he didn't speak.

It was up to her.

Fair enough. "For weeks now, I've wanted to tell you what I feel for you, in my heart. But I kept thinking I shouldn't rush things, shouldn't rush *you.* Or myself. I kept telling myself that it was too soon to start talking about the future, that now was the time to just be together, to let the future take care of itself. I reminded myself to enjoy being with you, to allow what we have to be… open-ended, I guess."

"Has it been so bad?" he asked, carefully. "Just being together, just taking every day as it comes?"

"Oh, no. Not bad." She felt the tears rise. And she gulped them back. "Far from it. It's been beautiful. Perfect…"

He was leaning toward her a little now. "So, then. Can we leave it at perfect? Why can't we do that?"

Because you are leaving me. And that is about as far from perfect as it gets….

She cleared her throat. "I just, well, I can sense that what we have together is not open-ended, not for you. You know what you're doing, *exactly* what you're doing.

You're giving me everything. Everything but the chance of a future with you. And today—which is the second day you haven't even put in an appearance on the project—today, for me, it all just got to be too much."

He tipped his head to the side, asked, "Is there a problem on the project?"

"No. Everything's going well. That's not what we're talking about."

"It *is* what we're talking about." He parsed out each syllable. "I'm available, if you need me. But you don't. You're up to speed. You can run this thing on your own."

She braced her elbows on the table and covered her face with her hands. "I'll ask you again. Is it the groundbreaking? Is that when you're going back to West Texas?"

There was only silence from his side of the table.

She lowered her hands and she stared straight at him. "Just tell me, Donovan. Is it the groundbreaking?"

And finally, slowly, he nodded. "Yeah. After the groundbreaking, I'm going back to West Texas."

"Without me," she said in a hollow whisper.

He gave her a slow, regal nod of his golden head. "Alone."

Her throat locked up. She looked away, coughed into her hand to try and clear it. The effort was pretty much a failure. When she spoke again, her voice was tight, ragged. "Why?" She faced him. "Oh, Donovan, what are you doing, just throwing it all away like this, throwing *us* away?"

His gaze was gentle. But he wasn't budging. "I told you. I told you that morning I wheeled in on you in the shower. I'm no good for this, no good for...love."

"And I told *you* that people can change."

"Not me. Not about this."

Her anger mounted. She tried to tamp it down. She spoke through tight lips, with measured care. "This is not about what you *can't* do, and you know it's not. It's simply that you *won't*. You won't move on from the horrible things that have happened to you, from the loss of Elias, from those days on the mountain, when death almost found you, but didn't. You're like Javier, you know that? Unforgiving. He can't forgive the woman he loves, even though that's the only way for him to find meaning in his life again. And you, Donovan—you can't forgive yourself."

His hands were on his wheels again, gripping tight. He continued in that so-patient, infuriating tone, "You're young and you're beautiful. And you're a fine architect. Exceptional. You're going to do great work. And someday you're going to find the right guy, a really good guy, a guy who's not all broken up inside and out. You'll settle down together, have children, build that special house of yours…."

It was too much. She wanted to jump up, start shouting, to try and get through to him by sheer volume, since nothing else seemed to work.

But she didn't jump up. She refused to raise her voice.

She stayed in that chair and she spoke with furious softness. "Don't you get it? I love *you,* Donovan. You *are* the right guy. I want my children to be *our* children. Don't you know that? I want to build that house for *us*."

He flinched as if she'd struck him. "Stop."

"But—"

"No more." He did back his chair from the table, then. But instead of turning and wheeling away, he jerked to a stop and told her flatly, "Never. No. I will never have another child. I couldn't do that, couldn't go through that again—and yes, I've been selfish. And wrong, to be with you, to give in to wanting you. I see that. I know it. I guess I knew it all along."

"Wrong?" She couldn't believe he'd actually said that. She did jump to her feet then. "Of course, it wasn't wrong. *This* is what's wrong."

"This." He glared up at her. "This…what?"

"This. You. Making my choices for me. *That's* wrong."

"I made no choices for you."

"Oh, yes you did. You decided to set everything up for me, to give me everything I've ever wanted, to make my life perfect for me—only without *you* in it. You decided that I wanted kids and you didn't, and then you decided that therefore it's impossible for things to work out with us."

He demanded, "Did you or did you not just say you wanted your kids to be my kids?"

"I only—"

"Answer me! Did you say it or not?"

"I did, yes. But nothing is absolute. It doesn't all *have* to turn out a certain way."

"Oh, right, Abilene. You go ahead. You tell me that you don't want to be the go-to architect for the children's center."

"I didn't say that."

"Tell me that you don't want children. Tell me that right to my face."

"Of course, I want children. But if *you* don't, well, we could at least talk about that."

He made a scoffing sound. "We could talk."

"Yes. Talk. Please."

His lip curled in a sneer. "What is there to talk about?"

"Plenty. Maybe I could live without kids. Did that ever occur to you? And even if I couldn't, how would you know what I can or can't get along without, if you haven't even asked me?"

He rolled back to the table. "All this is just so much noise. You have to know that."

"Noise? After all these weeks, we're finally talking, finally saying the things that need to be said—and you call it noise?"

"It's a waste of breath, to hash it out like this. Because it's not up for discussion. None of it is up for discussion. I was wrong, to get personally involved with you. I see that now."

She stared at him. The distance across that table seemed to be miles—endless, unbridgeable miles. Her knees felt all quivery. She sank back into the chair and asked, her voice breaking, "Wrong? You keep saying it was wrong. You really think that? That what we've had is wrong?"

"I've only hurt you."

"No. No, that's not true. You know it's not. Oh, why can't you see? We've had more, so much more than just this, just the hurting. And we could make a life, a *good* life. You know that we could. If you would only—"

"No."

"You keep saying that."

"Because you're not listening."

She was running out of arguments, running out of ways to try and get through to him. "Just...like that? Just, no?"

"I will be at the groundbreaking." His voice was quiet, resigned. "I'll play my part. And if I'm needed on the project, I'm there for it. But as for the rest of it…" He winced, turned his head away and stared off toward the bow window. It was dark out by then. All he could possibly see was his own ghostly reflection. "It's over. And it's time we accepted that."

It's over….

All the breath seemed to leave her body. She was empty. A shell. Finished in the worst, most final way. What more could she do? She had told him she loved him, that she wanted a life with him, a life on *his* terms.

And it had meant nothing to him.

Less than nothing.

He had denied her. He was sending her away.

And still, somewhere deep in her obstinate, hopeful heart, she wanted to fight for him. She did. She wanted to believe that if she could only find the right words, it would make all the difference, would make him admit that he loved her, make him beg her to stay.

But words had deserted her. And she didn't believe. Not anymore. He turned his gaze to her again.

She looked into his eyes and all she saw was a weariness to equal her own. The only thing left for her to say was, "I'll just get my stuff together, then."

Carefully, feeling as though she might shatter if she moved too fast, she pushed herself to her feet again. She put one foot in front of the other. She went out of the kitchen and down the hallway to his bedroom.

She took her clothes from the closet, went to the bathroom, got her toothbrush and hair dryer, her shampoo and her makeup. She packed it all up. When she had everything, she rolled the full suitcase back to the kitchen.

He was still sitting at the table. She was careful not to look directly at him as she got her tote from the chair where she'd dropped it, took out the key he had given her, and laid it on the counter.

He said nothing as she left him.

The silence between them was absolute.

Chapter Fourteen

For Abilene, the days that followed were a grueling exercise in concentration. She found that if she could manage to keep the focus on her work—and not on her battered heart—she got through the daylight hours well enough.

Nights were another story. She had trouble sleeping. And when she did drop off finally, Donovan's very absence seemed to weave through her dreams, where she wandered, lost and disoriented. And cold.

She would wake to find herself curled in a ball all the way over on the far side of the bed—*his* side of the bed. Seeking his body's warmth.

Seeking *him.*

Four days later, true to his word, Donovan attended the groundbreaking ceremony.

Abilene wished he hadn't. She was suffering enough, thank you very much. Seeing him, hearing his voice…

it only made the hurt sharper, made her poor heart ache all the harder.

He made a brief speech about the project—and about the brilliant young architect he had found to create the perfect space where children could have the chance they needed to learn and grow. He spoke from his wheelchair, using a wireless microphone, and he was as charming and inspiring as he had been all those years ago, the first time she saw him, when he came to give that talk at Rice.

Abilene thought he looked killer handsome, if a little tired—and then reminded herself that it shouldn't matter to her if he was tired. His well-being was not her problem. She'd been a fool ever to have imagined it was.

After the ceremony, a local gallery hosted a party in honor of the big day. Donovan put in an appearance. Abilene kept her distance from him and he steered clear of her, as well.

Her mom and dad were there, to celebrate her success with her. And three of her brothers and their wives showed up. And Zoe and Dax, too. They all knew that Abilene and Donovan were through. Out of respect for one of their own, they avoided him.

Except for Dax.

As the party was winding down, Abilene spotted the two men in an isolated corner of the gallery, speaking quietly to each other, both of them looking way too intense. Donovan glanced over and saw her watching.

Their gazes locked. She felt the floor drop out from under her, felt her heart tear in two all over again.

And then came the quick, flaring heat of her fury—at herself, for caring so damn much. At him, for turning his broad back on the best thing that had every happened to him.

She tore her gaze from his and turned away.

He left soon after that. She didn't ask Dax what he and Donovan had said to each other. She told herself she didn't want to know.

A week after the groundbreaking, Ruth Gilman offered her a position at Johnson Wallace. She accepted the job and also the great starting salary and nice benefit package.

And a week after she got her dream job, out of the blue, Ben Yates called. He said he'd kept her number and had been thinking about her.

At first, she was wary, afraid that maybe Donovan was using Ben to check up on her, to make sure she was taking full advantage of the "perfect" life he had set up for her. But Ben said he was living in Fort Worth and had managed to land a good job with a top firm. He said he hadn't spoken to Donovan since the day he walked out of the house in the desert.

And he told her that he'd been regretting the way he'd left, without even saying goodbye her.

"It's okay, Ben," she reassured him. "I understood why you had to go. And I'm happy that things seem to be working out for you."

"So, then. Good. And the children's center…"

"Under construction. I'm the supervising architect. And I'm at Johnson Wallace now."

"Congratulations. They're the best."

"Thanks. I love the job. It's working out well."

"So…are you seeing anyone? I was just thinking, if you're free some evening, I would catch a flight down to San Antonio. We could have dinner."

She really wanted to say yes. She liked Ben, so much. He was the kind of guy she'd always thought she would finally fall for. Fun to be with. A good guy, honest. Forthright. Without a lot of emotional baggage—completely unlike the man she was trying so hard to get over.

But she just couldn't do it, couldn't use Ben to try to forget Donovan. She needed to do the forgetting first.

And then maybe, someday, she would be ready for a guy like Ben.

So she laid the hard truth right out there. "I would like to be your friend, Ben. But that's all."

"I see," he said, softly. And then he thanked her for being honest with him. And he said he thought that maybe it was better, if they just let it go at that.

She hung up feeling a little sad, but grateful to have achieved something like closure with Ben. And she was also longing for Donovan.

She tried to remind herself that her broken heart would mend, that even the deepest hurt someday heals.

But the platitudes weren't helping. She loved him.

She missed him. She wished she could fast-forward time past the hurting and the yearning. She longed to be all the way over on the other side of heartbreak. To be at that moment when she could think of Donovan fondly, without that empty aching feeling, without wanting to wring his obstinate neck.

The next day, Ruth shared some gossip. She'd learned from a colleague at the Johnson Wallace Los Angeles office that Donovan had accepted a commission to design a theater complex in Century City. Abilene pasted on a smile at the news and said how fabulous that was for Century City.

And it *was* fabulous. Even if he couldn't accept love in his life, well, at least he was working again. That was something. That was important.

She would try to focus on that, on how he was living a productive life now. She would tell herself that maybe she'd had a little bit to do with that, with waking him up from his long, painful retreat into solitude and loneliness, with bringing him back to the world.

Did it help, to think that she might have helped *him?*

Not really.

In the end, she just had to set her mind on acceptance, on getting through the days away from him, on letting time do its job much too slowly, on telling herself that she was getting there, getting over Donovan McRae.

On the first Monday in April, Javier came to see her at Johnson Wallace. He told her that he had a client who wanted a house.

A very special house.

Javier said the client was a dear friend of his, a woman, a single mother with three children, a family law attorney. His friend wanted to adopt a fourth child. She planned to build her dream house for her family—and her three large dogs. She owned the property already, in the Hill Country—the perfect piece of land, with beautiful views.

He described what his friend wanted, how big the house should be, and the general arrangement of the rooms. Was Abilene interested?

Abilene almost said no automatically. Which was insane. She had a living to make. And she wouldn't get far if she started turning away potential clients, sight unseen.

And she *wasn't* turning down any clients. Her no had been merely a protective reaction. Because as Javier had described what the woman wanted, a chill had snaked its way down her spine.

Abilene knew that house.

It was *her* dream house.

The house that would always now, to her, be Donovan's house, too.

The house she needed to relinquished, because there was no way she would ever have it built to share with another man.

Javier asked, "So? What do you say?"

And she got it then. She saw that this could be an answer for her. Creating her dream house for Javier's friend and her family could be a big step in getting free of the pain, in letting her love for Donovan go.

She said, "Well, as it turns out, I have a house in mind, just from what you've told me. Something I've been tinkering with over the years. It's really pretty amazing, how close my design is to the house you just described."

"Ah," said Javier, the crinkles at the corners of his dark eyes deepening with his smile. "So maybe this is meant to be, huh? It's fate that you should design this special house."

"Well, I don't know about fate. But I'm definitely interested in meeting with your friend—and I wonder, is it possible for me to see the property first? I just want to make certain that the design I would propose is right for the setting." Okay, that was stretching the truth. What she really wanted was to reassure herself in advance that the property was right for the house.

And why shouldn't she want that? If she was going to give this single mom *her* dream house, well, it would have to be built on the ideal piece of land.

If the property didn't cut it, fine. She'd come up with something different for Javier's friend.

"I don't see why not," Javier said. "Let me call her, see if it's okay with her. And then I'll call you back."

Javier did call, the next morning.

He said his friend was excited at the idea that the architect needed to see the land first. In fact, his friend was hoping that maybe Abilene could meet her on the property. His friend would love to have the chance to show Abilene the spot where she wanted to put the house—a spot not far from the creek that ran through the property, with a view from the kitchen of a certain craggy peak, and from the master bedroom of a wide, open field, a field that was thick with Texas bluebonnets this time of year.

It seemed to Abilene a good omen for the project, that she and the prospective client viewed the process in a similar light. Abilene wanted to like Javier's friend, to be able to believe in the happiness that the woman and her family might find in the house.

So Abilene agreed to meet the client on the property. She gave Javier a couple of prospective meeting dates and times. He called back again later that day to say his friend would meet her the following morning at 11:00 a.m.

She laughed. "Don't you think it's about time you told me this woman's name?"

"Donna," he said. "Donna Rae."

Donna Rae.

Abilene felt that chill down her back again. Donna Rae?

It was just a little too close to Donovan, a little too much like McRae.

But really, she was being silly. The similarity between the two names was a coincidence, no more. She refused to get all freaked out because the woman's name reminded her of the man she couldn't seem to forget.

Javier said, "So then. I'll email you a map with directions to the property."

"Fair enough—and Javier, thank you for thinking of me. I'm excited about this, I really am."

"I'm glad," he said, his voice strangely somber. But then, Javier was too somber, too much of the time. "Call me tomorrow, after the meeting. Let me know...how it went."

She promised him that she would. And the next morning at nine-thirty, she was on her way.

It was a lovely ride. The Hill Country was beautiful any time, but never more so than now, in the spring, with wildflowers in bloom in every rolling, green field. She cranked the radio up loud and rolled her windows down.

At five to eleven, she turned onto the freshly paved road that would take her to the property. Live oaks lined the way, casting leafy shadows on the hood of her car as she sailed along. And beyond the screen of the trees, she could see open country, green and rolling and draped in a blanket of bluebonnets.

Yes, she thought. *This is exactly right. This is the place where my house should be.*

She slowed to make the turn onto the dirt driveway, stirring up dust as she rolled onto the unpaved surface. Limestone outcroppings flanked the way to either side and she was aware of the rising feeling of her own anticipation. She was almost there.

She rounded a gentle curve, saw the cleared space, the van parked and waiting.

And Donovan standing beside it.

Chapter Fifteen

Fury. Longing. Hope. Joy.

The burning desire to make him pay…

A hot, knotted tangle of emotions warred within her, sending her heart rocketing beneath her breastbone, making her palms sweat, causing her knees to quiver at the very idea she might have to use them to stand upright.

Upright. Like he was.

It was the first time she'd ever seen him up on his own two feet—well, okay, he was kind of leaning against the side of the van, and his wheelchair was right there, behind him. Ready in case he needed it.

But still. He *was* standing. How wonderful.

If only she didn't want to kill him, she would be so proud of him.

He continued to lean there, against the side of the van, as if he had all the time in the world to stand there and stare at her through the windshield of her car.

She couldn't read his expression. He only *looked* at her. What was going through that frustrating mind of his? She shouldn't even want to know.

But there was no point in lying to herself. She did want to know. She *needed* to know. As much as she needed to draw her next breath.

And speaking of her breath…

It had clogged in her throat. Slowly, with care, she let it out. And then breathed in again, a conscious action. And out. And in.

Great. She was making real progress here. She could breathe again.

And her heart was still beating much too fast, but at least it had slowed down a little bit. It had stopped galloping along like a spooked horse. She felt almost certain her legs would hold her up now if she tried to stand on them.

So she pushed open her door, swung her feet to the ground and got out of the car. "Donna Rae," she said flatly. "A single mom, huh? A single mom with three kids—and a plan to adopt a fourth. A family lawyer, with three big dogs? Don't try and tell me Javier dreamed all that up."

He straightened, so his legs took his full weight. "Don't blame Javier. It was me. All me."

Down a slope of land, she could hear water rushing over rocks—a creek. She could see it, gleaming there, beneath the trees. And that craggy peak Javier had mentioned—yes, she saw it, too. Right where it should be, off in the middle distance, perfect for framing in a kitchen window.

She made herself look at Donovan. And she ached to go to him.

No way.

She broadened her stance a fraction, settling herself in place, and folded her hands protectively over her middle. "Oh, I'm killing Javier, too. Just as soon as I finish with you."

He put up both hands, palms out. Surrender. "I only…I didn't know if you would speak to me."

"How about a phone call? That's always a viable way to start."

"I was afraid you would hang up."

"I probably would have. Then you could have called again. And again. That would have been satisfying."

He took one step. And another. She watched in wonder. And in fierce, injured fury, as well. "I knew I had really screwed up with you. Screwed up so bad."

"No argument there."

"I knew that just telling you I love you, confessing that I was wrong, that all I wanted was another chance…" He took that last step. He was two feet away from her. The clean scent of him taunted her. And he was tanner than before. His hair gleamed, pure gold, in the spring sunlight. And her arms ached to reach for him. Her throat ached to speak her love.

And her heart ached most of all.

She only wanted to grab him, to pull him to her, to hold him fast and never, ever let him go.

She kept her arms around herself instead. And she taunted him, "So you cooked up some big lie and got Javier to help you with it."

His strong jaw twitched. And he shifted, wincing. Evidently it still wasn't that easy for him to get around on his damaged legs. "Okay, it was a stupid idea. I should have just called you, I see that now. But I wanted…I *needed* for you to know that I'm not here just to talk. That I want you so much. I love you…so much."

"Love?" She could choke on that word. "You have no right. No right at all, to talk to me about love."

"I know. I get it. I do. I was a complete fool to have let you go. And so I thought that maybe, if you saw that I wanted to hire Javier to build your house, you would listen to me. You would believe that I've actually come to my senses. You would listen to me when I say that what I really want, more than anything, is to be the man who lives in that house with you..."

The tears rose, clogging her throat all over again. She willed them away. But they wouldn't go. They spilled over and slid down her face.

She swiped them away, furious that they wouldn't stop.

"Abilene." His voice was rough with emotion. "Come on. Don't cry." He started to reach for her.

She jerked back. "Don't you dare. You just keep those hands of yours to yourself."

He obeyed, even moved back a step and let his arms fall to his sides. "It's been...really bad. Without you."

Triumph surged within her. She knew it was petty, to feel glad that he had been suffering, too. But she did feel glad.

God help her. She did.

A sob escaped her. She swallowed it down, swiped at the tears again. "I thought it was what you wanted, to be without me. You said it was what you wanted. You said love was not an option, that you were no good when it came to forever."

"I was an idiot."

She almost laughed. But somehow, it came out as another sob. "Yeah. Yeah, you were. You definitely were." She put her hands to her cheeks, rubbed more of the wetness away.

His eyes were so tender, so full of regret. "I hate that I hurt you. I...didn't realize..." The sentence trailed off. He looked away, off toward the sloping of the land and the gleam of the creek.

She sniffed. "What, Donovan? You didn't realize, what?"

And he turned to her again. "I didn't realize that after you, after what we had together, there was no way I could go back to hiding in the desert. Back to the silence and the pain and the guilt over Elias. I don't think I'm ever going to be capable of forgiving myself for not protecting him, for not taking better care of him. But I am learning that I need to move on."

She felt her fury leaving her. She couldn't hold on to it. Her anger was nothing when measured against the love that still lived in her heart. And the tenderness in his eyes.

He said, "I finally get it. I do. It's what you tried so hard to get me to see. That I didn't die, after all. That I owe it to Elias's memory, to pick up the pieces, to do whatever I can to make the world a better place for *all* the children."

Her mouth trembled. She caught her lower lip between her teeth to still it. "I heard...that you were working again. I was glad for that. Truly."

He nodded. "My old literary agent called, offered me a new book contract. She wanted me to write the story of how I came back from near-death on Dhaulagiri One."

"And?"

His broad shoulders lifted in a shrug. "I passed on that. Maybe someday. But not now. Not so soon."

"Ruth told me, about the theater complex in Century City."

"Yeah. It's a complex that will include a children's

theater and a place for kids to come to practice stagecraft, to get their first chance onstage. And after that, I'll be designing a preschool in Portland, Oregon."

"That's good," she said. "I'm really happy for you."

And then he said it again. "I love you, Abilene."

She only looked at him. Stricken. Yearning. Wanting to say she loved him, too. Wanting that with all her heart. And yet… "You hurt me. You hurt me so bad…."

His gaze didn't waver. "I know it. That I hurt you. That I don't deserve you. I know that I've given you a lot more grief than happiness in the time we had together. But please. Just consider coming back to me. Just think about it. If you give me one more chance, I swear to you, I won't blow it this time. I'll spend the rest of my life proving that I can be the man you always hoped I could be."

She turned away from him, unable, somehow, to look in his eyes at that moment. She made herself ask him, "And the children, Donovan? What about the children? What about *our* children? Because I've had time to think about it, too, about what I want, about what I *don't* want to live without. And you were right about that, if nothing else. I do want children. I want them a lot."

He did touch her then. He took that one step closer and he put his warm hands on her shoulders. She felt his breath stir her hair and she trembled.

"I know that," he said. "I always knew."

She stared off toward the craggy peak. It shone silvery in the sunlight. "And?"

He dared to move in closer still, to clasp her shoulders more firmly. She felt his touch to the core of her and she sighed. He bent close. His lips brushed her temple, burning.

And he whispered, "I'm willing."

She gasped, whirled to face him once more, searched his eyes, wanting, needing, to know the truth. "You mean that? You're willing to be a father…again?"

He gave one slow nod of that golden head. "I know I'll be overprotective. And the whole idea of having more kids scares the hell out of me. It's not as if I'll ever be that fast on my feet, you know? And children, they need a dad who's fast on his feet."

Her tears spilled over again. She gave up fighting them. Unashamed, she let them trail down her face. "Children need a dad who loves them. That's what they really need."

He touched her cheek, smeared her tear tracks with his thumb. "Say yes," he whispered prayerfully.

She couldn't. Not yet. But she did say, "If we had children, I would be there, right beside you, whenever you needed me. And it doesn't hurt a child to learn to be a little self-sufficient. If you love them enough, if you teach them well, I don't even know that you have to be that fast on your feet."

He studied her upturned face, hungrily. Tenderly. "I love you, Abilene. You gave me back my work. You gave me everything. You made me hope again. You made me *live* again. And these last rotten weeks, without you… well, I see it now. I get it. You're what makes it all complete. And I swear I would get down on my knees to you, right now, here, in the dirt. If I only thought I had a prayer of getting back up again."

A torn laugh escaped her. "Oh, Donovan."

"Please. Say it. Tell me it's not too late."

She lifted on tiptoe, put her hands against his chest, felt his strength and his warmth and the beating of his heart. "You have to be sure. Absolutely sure."

"I am. Say yes."

She hesitated on the brink. "I didn't want to keep loving you…."

"Say yes."

She smiled through her tears. "But I did. I do. It's you, Donovan. Only you."

"Abilene. Thank God." He gathered her close, lowered his mouth to hers.

The kiss they shared held everything: their love, their sworn commitment, each to the other—and more. That kiss held the promise of the future they would share, including the house they would build on that very spot, with the craggy peak out the kitchen window, the field of bluebonnets and the clear, cool creek down the slope in back.

Their children would grow strong and tall there. And it seemed to her that the bold, brave spirit of the lost Elias would be with them always, too.

When he lifted his head, he said, "Marry me."

She gave him the answer her heart had been holding, just for him: "Yes."

He took her hand. "Come on. Let me show you how I picture it—your house."

"*Our* house," she reminded him.

"Yeah. That sounds good. That sounds right. *Our* house. Let me show you…."

"I can see it already." She beamed up at him. "But show me, anyway."

* * * * *

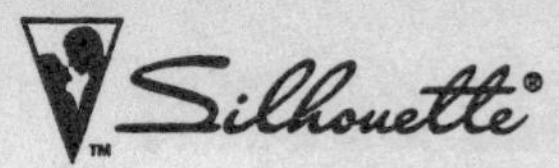

SPECIAL EDITION®

COMING NEXT MONTH

Available February 22, 2011

#2101 MARRIAGE, BRAVO STYLE!
Christine Rimmer
Bravo Family Ties

#2102 MENDOZA'S RETURN
Susan Crosby
The Fortunes of Texas: Lost...and Found

#2103 TAMING THE TEXAS PLAYBOY
Crystal Green
Billionaire Cowboys, Inc.

#2104 HIS TEXAS WILDFLOWER
Stella Bagwell
Men of the West

#2105 SOMETHING UNEXPECTED
Wendy Warren
Home Sweet Honeyford

#2106 THE MILLIONAIRE'S WISH
Abigail Strom

SSECNM0211

USA TODAY *bestselling author Lynne Graham*
is back with a thrilling new trilogy
SECRETLY PREGNANT, CONVENIENTLY WED

Three heroines must marry alpha males to keep their dreams...but Alejandro, Angelo and Cesario are not about to be tamed!

Book 1—JEMIMA'S SECRET
Available March 2011 from Harlequin Presents®.

JEMIMA yanked open a drawer in the sideboard to find Alfie's birth certificate. Her son was her husband's child. It was a question of telling the truth whether she liked it or not. She extended the certificate to Alejandro.

"This has to be nonsense," Alejandro asserted.

"Well, if you can find some other way of explaining how I managed to give birth by that date and Alfie not be yours, I'd like to hear it," Jemima challenged.

Alejandro glanced up, golden eyes bright as blades and as dangerous. "All this proves is that you must still have been pregnant when you walked out on our marriage. It does not automatically follow that the child is mine."

"'I know it doesn't suit you to hear this news now and I really didn't want to tell you. But I can't lie to you about it. Someday Alfie may want to look you up and get acquainted."

"If what you have just told me is the truth, if that little boy does prove to be mine, it was vindictive and extremely selfish of you to leave me in ignorance!"

Jemima paled. "When I left you, I had no idea that I was still pregnant."

"Two years is a long period of time, yet you made no attempt to inform me that I might be a father. I will want DNA tests to confirm your claim before I make any deci-

HPEXP0311

sion about what I want to do."

"Do as you like," she told him curtly. "*I* know who Alfie's father is and there has never been any doubt of his identity."

"I will make arrangements for the tests to be carried out and I will see you again when the result is available," Alejandro drawled with lashings of dark Spanish masculine reserve.

"I'll contact a solicitor and start the divorce," Jemima proffered in turn.

Alejandro's eyes narrowed in a piercing scrutiny that made her uncomfortable. "It would be foolish to do anything before we have that DNA result."

"I disagree," Jemima flashed back. "I should have applied for a divorce the minute I left you!"

Alejandro quirked an ebony brow. "And why didn't you?"

Jemima dealt him a fulminating glance but said nothing, merely moving past him to open her front door in a blunt invitation for him to leave.

"I'll be in touch," he delivered on the doorstep.

What is Alejandro's next move? Perhaps rekindling their marriage is the only solution! But will Jemima agree?

Find out in Lynne Graham's
exciting new romance
JEMIMA'S SECRET

Available March 2011
from Harlequin Presents®.

HPEXP0311